FELLOW PASSENGERS

A Novel
in Portraits

D0959672

LOUIS AUCHINCLOSS

ST. MARTIN'S PAPERBACKS

The quotation on page vii is from Harold Nicolson's *Some People*, copyright © 1982 by Nigel Nicolson, and is reprinted with the permission of Atheneum Publishers, an imprint of Macmillan Publishing Company. The verses on page 75 are from *The Collected Poems of A. E. Housman*, copyright 1939, 1940, © 1965 by Holt, Rinehart and Winston, Inc., copyright © 1967, 1968 by Robert E. Symons, and are reprinted by permission of Henry Holt and Company, Inc.

Published by arrangement with Houghton Mifflin

FELLOW PASSENGERS

Copyright © 1989 by Louis Auchincloss.

Library of Congress Catalog Card Number: 88-23099

ISBN: 0-312-92391-0

Printed in the United States of America

Houghton Mifflin edition published 1989
St. Martin's Paperbacks edition/January 1991

10 9 8 7 6 5 4 3 2 1

I use the same foreword that Harold Nicolson used for his *Some People*, which gave me my conception for this collection:

Many of the following sketches are purely imaginary. Such truths as they may contain are only half-truths.

Contents

FELLOW PASSENGERS

Aunt Mabel

FROM MY TWELFTH to my fifteenth year, in the early 1930s, my parents used to rent a cottage for the summer in Bar Harbor, on beautiful Mount Desert Island just off the Maine coast. Sometimes, when my older brother, Jasper, was in camp, and Father had been called back to New York on business and Mother chose to go with him, I would be sent over to "Bonniecrest" to stay with my Ruggles grandparents. Their Maine summer was longer than ours; it began punctually on the second Monday of June and ended on the second Monday of September. Once I remained until the final day, coming down with them on the Bar Harbor Express, after having observed with curiosity the elaborate final cleaning and dusting of the whole establishment, the enshrouding of furniture in slipcovers, the hammering in of storm windows, and the enveloping of sentimental garden statuary in wooden crates.

Father used to make fun of the rigor of his parents' routine (though never to their faces), but I secretly admired it. I liked the hushed atmosphere of the asymmetrical shingle villa, humped atop a small hill and surrounded by woods, except where a cut provided a dazzling view from the verandah of Frenchman's Bay. I loved the big clean airy rooms, the matted floors, the heavy mahogany chairs, and the old Irish maidservants, who crept in when Grandmother rang for them (she never hollered, as Mother did). I liked sitting in the dark library with Grandpa, a huge, silent, friendly man, with a rumbling laugh and a round pot, who never did a stroke of exercise (unless fishing be called that) and sat inside all day until his afternoon drive with Grandmother in a hired Packard touring car driven by a youth from the Bar Harbor Motor Company. He had shelves of large illustrated volumes about the families and mistresses of French kings, which he and I both read with relish, exchanging occasional comments, when my high tones must have offered a funny contrast to his gravelly mutterings. But it was delightful not to have Mother barging in and exclaiming, "How can you sit inside on a lovely day like this? What's the point of taking you to Maine if this is all you do? And what are you reading? *An Infamous Regent's Rule?* What tosh! Go out at once and practice your forehand against the backboard."

Grandpa, to his family and household, and except in occasional temper tantrums, was something of a cipher; it was his wife who, in her quiet, ineluctable way, dominated the interior. She suffered from something that she called nervous tension, and she had, years before, become a convert to the famous rest cures of the novelist-psychiatrist S. Weir Mitchell. The reason for the finger-on-the-lips silence that pervaded Bonniecrest was that Grandmother, at almost any odd hour of the day, might be lying down in her bedroom with the shades pulled. She was small and dignified, with a charming soft laugh, and had been supposed to be something of a beauty in her youth. But she and Mother, though outwardly on the best of terms, were not truly sympathetic. I had heard enough of my parents' conversations at home to have gleaned that Mother did not share the Ruggles family's sympathy for Grandmother's frail health, which she regarded as the symptom of a chronic valetudinarianism.

There was an episode to which Mother often mysteriously referred as the cold beam of light that had at last revealed the sacrosanct Julia Ruggles to her son. Ultimately I made out that it was this: Father in the summer of 1920 had been taken in as a partner of his law firm. But when he wrote to his parents, then in Maine, to give them this jubilant news, there had been no response. Meeting their train at Grand Central that September, he had inquired dryly if they had not received his letter. "Oh yes, my dear boy," his mother had replied, "and we were so proud! But it was the time of that terrible bomb attack on Morgan's, and your father and I were too upset to answer any of our correspondence." The blast from the mysterious wagon parked outside 23 Wall Street had actually shattered the window of the office where Father had been working, twenty stories above. But as Mother never failed to remind him, it had not reached as far as Maine.

Children are quick to take advantage of a situation, and I found it fun to irritate Mother by parading my affection and admiration for Grandmother, divining that as a loyal in-law she could not openly deprecate this. And in truth some of my feeling was genuine. Although I was quite aware that Grandmother's interest in my little affairs, however civil, had a perfunctory quality, it fascinated me to hear her talk of her own distant childhood, and it thrilled my developing historical imagination when she told the story of how she had heard, at the age of eight, sitting in the children's dining room of her father's Fifth Avenue brownstone, the piercing Irish wails from below stairs: "Mr. Lincoln is shot! Mr. Lincoln is dead!" Then, too, an early snobbish instinct helped me to make out from her discourse the fact that her family, the Leroys, had been in their day much sweller and "older New York" than the Ruggleses, or than Mother's family, the Fishers. And it struck me as rather splendid that she should have preserved all their ancient prejudices intact and taken quite for granted that Mrs. Gould Bell, the smartest hostess on the island, would have given up her four-masted schooner to be invited to what I had once overheard Mother describe as Grandmother's "dowdy" dinner parties. Yet even at my tender age I suspected that Mrs. Bell was not even aware of Grandmother or of the fact that, as a divorcée, she would not have been welcome at Bonniecrest.

There were exceptions to Grandmother's rule. Uncle Jonathan, Father's older brother, had been divorced. But then, as Mother used to say, Uncle Jonathan was the only person whom Grandmother ever really loved. It seemed a curious preference. Uncle Jonathan's nickname at Yale had been "Stiffy," and never was a sobriquet more appropriate. He was a ramrod of a man, with a huge sharp nose, straight hair slicked back over his high dome, and suits that never showed a wrinkle. He gave an air of importance to his least actions, hiking up his trousers as he sat down, perching his pince-nez carefully on the thin bridge of his nose, uttering loud introductory coughs before even the most banal remark, or giving vent to the bray of a laugh whose very friendliness was intended to make up for the fact that it was all the friendliness one was going to get from him. Uncle Jonathan had been married to a beautiful and frivolous lady who twenty years before had fled in horror from him, and their daughter, now adult, was living in Paris under circumstances not revealed to me but evidently reprehensible, as for once Mother and Grandmother agreed on a subject.

Uncle Jonathan, at any rate, seemed never to have shown the least interest in remarrying, and he had long lived as a confirmed bachelor with his parents in New York and Maine. In town he was a banker of sorts and dined every night at a single table at the Union Club. Father, who clung all his life to the resentments of a kid brother who had been obliged to shine the shoes of his mother's favorite, never missed the chance, even under his wife's warning eye, to insinuate, with a wink and a chuckle, that "Stiffy" made long visits to the Union Club bar and shorter ones to certain unmentionable female establishments. This was not really like Father, but sibling rivalries do strange things to even the most generous-minded people.

Uncle Jonathan and I, during my visits to his parents, maintained a formal relationship, but one perfectly satisfactory to each. He approved of children who asked nothing of him. "Hello there, young fellow," he would boom out when I appeared at the breakfast table, "what sort of mischief are you planning today?" And that would pretty well do it for another twenty-four hours. I shared with Grandpa the court at Versailles and with Grandmother the tales of old Manhattan. But greater warmth was not altogether lacking at Bonniecrest. There was Aunt Mabel, Father's younger sister, whose love of everyone filled the house whenever she came.

The term "maiden aunt" is today considered a pejorative one, and so it was in my boyhood. But if people hadn't said it, they would have thought it. For although Aunt Mabel was as naturally cheerful and as spontaneously kind as Uncle Jonathan was falsely hearty and self-absorbed, although she was more charitable and public-spirited than any other member of the family, there was still a note of condescension even in the warmest encomiums that her relatives accorded her. Aunt Mabel at forty-plus was not now going to marry and have children, and that was what the Ruggleses, including my indubitably intelligent mother, considered the essential function of a woman. If she didn't do *that*, the implication seemed to be, she could jolly well stay home and look after the old folks, a fate that poor Aunt Mabel appeared docilely to accept. In New York, it was true, she worked five days a week at a settlement house and sometimes dined with her old-maid friends, but she was always on call if Grandmother needed her, and in the long Maine summers she provided most of the slim diversion her parents had.

She was supposed to have been briefly pretty as a young woman, but I remember her with a round, pleasant, rather undistinguished countenance, innocent of any make-up, and thick dark hair that was never waved, in accordance with Grandmother's theory that "permanents" dimmed the "natural luster" of one's locks. But when she laughed, which she often did, the skin of her face had a charming way of crinkling up, and the infectious rumble of her chuckle was beguiling.

She was, in short, the best-natured creature in the world. She treated children as adults and adults sometimes as children; nothing seemed to curb her persistent good will and optimism. Why had no man married her? According to Father, two very attractive men (who later were successful on Wall Street) had wanted to, but Aunt Mabel, each time in a flurry of nerves, had not been able to make up her mind. Mother always maintained that Grandmother had failed in her job of steadying her through these crises, but then Grandmother never took responsibility for anyone, even for Uncle Jonathan.

Aunt Mabel offered me the kind of companionship that any child with constantly overseeing parents wants: she listened and laughed and applauded without seeming to find it necessary to correct or improve. On our walks on the "mountains" (really hills) of Mount Desert — expeditions in which, disliking all organized athletics, I reveled — she would smile pleasantly as I no doubt bored her with episodes of French court history that I had read with Grandpa. Her mild ruminations would be limited to "Gosh, for a thirteen-year-old you're quite a whiz in history, aren't you?" or "Do you think you might like to teach when you grow up?" But these were enough to satisfy me.

On these walks I used to create fantasies in which Mount Desert Island became a kingdom independent of the hostile "Mainland," and the visiting units of the U.S. Navy, viewed at anchor in the harbor from the top of Cadillac Mountain, were an invading enemy flotilla. I did not consider such daydreaming really worthy of a student of history, and I would have bit off my tongue before sharing it with anyone else. But Aunt Mabel was somehow different, and when I pointed to the gray hulk of the battleship *New York*, its formidability dwindled to a toy model, and identified it as the flagship of the hostile armada, she joined in the game with a zest which, although it did not meet my mood (I learned at once that such fantasies, by their very nature, are unshareable), in no way humiliated me. She exclaimed, "Yes, and I can see by the dragon pennant that the old dowager queen mother is on board! They must have carried her in her golden palanquin up to the bridge so she can gloat over the bombardment of her native town. For she was born a princess of Mount Desert, you know, and never forgave her parents for selling her to the monarch of Maine."

When my parents came up for a late summer weekend at Bonniecrest, having closed their own cottage for the season, it surprised me to note how Aunt Mabel seemed to defer to Mother. She and Father were apt to revert to the joshing, scrapping relationship of their earlier years, but with Mother she was much more serious and was inclined to discuss such topics as fund raising for her settlement house or what courses it might be interesting to take that fall at Columbia. This, I suspect, was not only because Mother was more broad-minded than any of the Ruggleses. It was because she took Aunt Mabel seriously as a human being. The fact that she partially shared the family feeling that Aunt Mabel had missed her main goal in life did not mean that her life had to be barren or dull. Mother was anxious that Aunt Mabel should make the best of what she had left.

That she was actually helping Aunt Mabel to hatch a career came out in the late August of 1932. It was revealed during the crisis occasioned by Uncle Jonathan's unexpected descent to New York and his almost immediate return, accompanied by his staid, elderly, long-suffering secretary, Miss Fenno, whom he put up in a hotel in the village. Word had reached him of the desperate illness from pneumonia of his daughter, Cynthia, in Paris, and foreseeing that his family would expect him to hurry at once to her bedside, he retired to the isolation of his chamber, from which he dispatched Miss Fenno with dictated memos to his parents and mine and to Aunt Mabel. Miss Fenno would then take their dictated answers back to him. It was an extraordinary performance.

Anxious to know what was going on, I cornered Aunt Mabel in Grandmother's garden where she was cutting damask roses and demanded if I wasn't old enough to be told. She straightened up and gazed thoughtfully at her shears.

"Why, yes, I guess so, honey. The trouble is that we all think your Uncle Jonathan should go over, and he won't."

"Why won't he?"

"Because he disapproves of the way Cynthia's living. She shares a flat with a man." Aunt Mabel faced me now with a look that made me feel very grown-up indeed. "A man she's not married to."

I puckered my brow in what I hoped was the frown of a man of the world. "Why don't they marry?"

"Because he has a wife." Here Aunt Mabel actually winked at me. "And one who won't give him a divorce. So they'll have to wait till he's a widower. Only that doesn't seem very likely. Actually, I'm afraid it may be the other way round. For he's got pneumonia, too."

"What do Father and Mother think?"

"Oh, they think Uncle Jonathan should go. We all do. It's no time for making moral judgments. They're getting very mad at him."

"You, too?"

"Well, I don't see the point. People are what they are. Jonathan won't go, and that's that. How does it help to get mad?"

Nothing could have more intensified my sense of being treated as an equal than her referring to Uncle Jonathan simply by his Christian name. I was at once transported into her world, and I even seemed to make out that behind the façade of Aunt Mabel's buoyancy, behind what I had once heard Father slightingly describe as her "girl scoutism," there might exist an assessment of the great world quite as shrewd and realistic as his own. The sudden dark, almost fatigued look in her soft brown eyes made me surmise that she, too, knew that history — real history, that is, not just Gallic court mistresses — could be horror, like the fate of all those millions of men, not much younger than Father, whose death in rat-ridden trenches at the time of my birth so strangely haunted my imagination. Oh, yes, I was suddenly sure that Aunt Mabel knew about those things. And even more.

That night after dinner Uncle Jonathan descended at last from his room, and there was a heated discussion in the living room. My presence in the library adjoining was completely overlooked, so I was able to hear every word of it. I was particularly struck by Father's emphatic tone. Although rather sharply critical of his parents and older brother at home, he was inclined to be subdued, or at least noncommittal, in their presence. I can see now that what he could not resist was this rare chance to prove to his doting mother that her oldest son had feet of clay. Feet? Uncle Jonathan seemed made of the substance.

Here is how I recall their voices.

UNCLE JONATHAN: It's all very well, Joe, for you and Lina to talk about parental duties transcending Christian principles, but your two boys are too young to have got into the kind of mess Cynthia's in. If she and her paramour were not actually under the same roof, if they were even in a hospital, in separate wards, I might be able to visit her without seeming to sanction their intrigue. But this way it's out of the question. Cynthia has made her bed. She'll have to lie in it.

GRANDMOTHER: I think, dear, you might have used another metaphor.

FATHER: He certainly might! Have you stopped to consider, Jonathan, how you'll feel if Cynthia actually dies over there?

UNCLE JONATHAN: I'm only concerned with her immortal soul. Not who is or isn't present at her passing. I wouldn't care if she died if I believed her soul was saved.

FATHER (*angrily*): You mean you wouldn't care if she died!

AUNT MABEL: Joe! You're going too far.

GRANDMOTHER: You certainly are, Joe.

UNCLE JONATHAN: Well, if you all feel so passionately about it, why doesn't one of *you* go over?

MOTHER: Very well. Shall we go, Joe?

FATHER: And give up the meeting of the Bar Association in Chicago? What are you thinking of, Lina? You know I'm chairman of the session on corporate bonds.

MOTHER: That's no reason I can't go, then.

FATHER: But I need you to run the firm's reception at the Drake! Really, Jonathan, how can you have the gall to expect your sister-in-law to do your job?

GRANDMOTHER: Then I'll go!

(*General consternation*)

GRANDFATHER (*his sole contribution*): Your health won't permit it, Julia. It's out of the question. And it's my place to be here, looking after you.

AUNT MABEL: Well, that seems to leave me.

FATHER: Actually, you might combine it with a bit of vacation, Mabel. Paris is nice in the fall, after the tourists have gone. And I'll be glad to blow you to a trip afterward, to London or Rome or wherever you want.

MOTHER: Your sister shouldn't be going on vacation now, Joe. Mabel has been taking some pre-nursing courses. She plans to enter Bellevue Nurses School in October. It wouldn't be right to ask her to put it off.

(*Further general consternation*)

GRANDMOTHER: But Mabel, dear, you never told me!

AUNT MABEL (*much flustered*): I was going to, Mother, next week. I wanted to prepare you for it first.

GRANDMOTHER: But, darling, aren't you too old?

AUNT MABEL: I guess I'll be the oldest in the class by ten or fifteen years, but so long as they don't mind . . .

UNCLE JONATHAN: If Mabel's been taking courses in nursing, why doesn't that make her the obvious person to go to Paris?

GRANDMOTHER: Dear me, a nurse. A trained nurse. This is very sudden. Do we know anyone who's a nurse? Can a lady really be one?

FATHER: What about Florence Nightingale?

GRANDMOTHER: But that was different, wasn't it? There was a war. I trust, Mabel, that you wouldn't hire out to go to people's houses? I'm sure Miss Nightingale didn't do that.

AUNT MABEL: No, Mother, I'll stick to hospital work, if that makes you feel any better about it.

It was obvious now to me that Aunt Mabel was going to Paris and that even Mother would not be able to prevent it. And go she did, remaining for two months in the city of light, largely in Cynthia's darkened chamber, and pulling her through, though not her less fortunate "paramour," who died. The reward for her good deed was the delay by a year of her admission to Bellevue Nurses School. I found the family's calm acceptance of her sacrifice outrageous and expressed myself sharply in a letter to Mother from Chelton School in Massachusetts, where I was now a second-former. She responded more temperately than I would have expected from Aunt Mabel's champion.

"You mustn't forget, dear, that what Aunt Mabel did

was really a part of the career she is planning to embrace. You say your grandparents or Uncle Jonathan should have gone, but wouldn't they really have been more of a hindrance than a help?"

It was like Mother not to criticize Father's excuse for not going to Paris. As to many women of her generation, anything concerning his work, the "sacred office," was given an undisputed priority. Mother never considered men superior to women; indeed, she may have believed just the reverse, but she had a respect for "downtown" as the source of her revenue, and this had little to do with the mere chance that men were in charge there. In placing Father's law practice leagues ahead of Aunt Mabel's nursing she was being realistic rather than antifeminist.

The following summer, Aunt Mabel's last before enrolling in her nursing school, Father and Mother invited her to go with us to a ranch in Jackson Hole. Our trip was not a success. Mother, away from what she deemed the security of city pavements and summer spas, became an almost irrational person, giving in shamelessly to her nervous anxiety over the supposed dangers of the Wyoming wilderness, and Father, who could never bear to see the misery in her very expressive eyes, would not oppose her. The result was that our rides were confined to the immediate vicinity of the ranch and on the oldest and sleepiest horses, and that no overnight excursions, "pack trips," were even considered. I found myself the butt of the jokes of the other boys at the ranch and was thoroughly miserable.

I did, however, make one effort to struggle out of the net of maternal restrictions. Aunt Mabel and I used to ride together ahead of our little group. Following Father's directions, she would make valiant attempts to "sit the trot," but it jostled her painfully, and she looked sadly dumpy and pathetic. I urged her to give it up.

"But your pa tells me that everyone out here does. He says they'd get too tired on day-long rides if they posted."

"And when do we take day-long rides, I'd like to know?"

"But that's perfectly true! Why didn't I think of it? Bless you, my boy." And she started comfortably posting as we trotted ahead.

"Don't you think, Aunt Mabel, it's a terrible waste of money for us to come all the way out here and not go on a single pack trip?"

"Well, it's hardly a waste of mine, since your father's paying for it."

"But a waste of his, then. All the kids say the whole point of the ranch is taking pack trips. Sleeping out under the stars and prowling down to the edge of a lake at dawn. It's the only way to see moose or elk. Or even a grizzly!"

"Heavens. Do we really want that?" She laughed, but I thought I could detect a shiver in her laugh.

"Oh, they never attack, except in the mating season."

"But how can you be sure when that is? Some randy old male might not know it was over."

"Oh, it's perfectly definite." I cursed myself for having

mentioned the silly beast. "Mr. and Mrs. Truex are going on one this Friday with their five kids. Their guide, Bill, says he can take two more. How about you and me going along?"

"Have you asked your mother?"

"Not yet. I wanted to get it all planned first. I know she thinks a lot of Mr. Truex. His firm is even bigger than Father's and he's the senior partner!"

Mr. Truex was indeed a considerable figure on the Wall Street of that day. Aunt Mabel seemed impressed.

"Gee, Dan, I guess it would be fun! I wasn't going to say anything about it to your father because he was kind enough to bring me along, but my friend, Dora Barney, told me that the pack trip she went on three summers ago was the greatest thing she'd ever done in her life. She almost saw a mountain goat. That is, the guide saw one. I suppose I shouldn't say it, but it does sometimes strike me that poor Lina worries about things that aren't really worth that much fuss. I'll talk to Mrs. Truex tonight."

I knew, hearing Aunt Mabel refer to Mother simply as "Lina," that I had again entered the mysterious world of adults.

Mrs. Truex spoke to Father, and he was bold enough to approve the trip, but my triumph was short-lived. His resolution did not long survive the sad, reproachful tone that Mother adopted when she was determined to get her way.

"Do you realize, Joe, that there's no doctor on that trip? And don't tell me that Mabel knows nursing; she's not even in school yet. Supposing Dan had appendicitis? What chance would they have to get him out alive, strapped to a jogging horse? Or supposing he fell off his horse and had a concussion, and there they were, miles from nowhere? It just doesn't make sense to take that sort of risk with a child's life!"

I think I actually hated Mother at that moment. I can almost hate her, poor afflicted woman though I know she was, when I think of it now.

Yet Mother, even restored to the sanctuary of Manhattan, refused to express the least apology for having ruined everyone's summer. So strongly did she believe in life — in the lives, that is, of her two sons — and so unimportant did she consider all activities and sports with the least built-in danger, such as sailing, aviating, hunting, or even skiing, that she never blamed herself for limiting, or even curtailing altogether, our involvement in them. When in later years I would point out to her that she had paid a certain price in the apprehensiveness that her constant worrying had engendered in our psyches, she would simply retort, "Well, you're alive, aren't you? And not dead like your cousin Willy in that skiing accident on Mount Washington or the Bradley boy who wanted to be a flier?"

What could one say to an argument like that?

When, on my next Christmas vacation, I brought up, rather naggingly, the subject of the pack trip veto, and argued that even if she had had the right to deprive me of it, she had had none to deprive Aunt Mabel, she surprised me by retorting that Aunt Mabel had felt just as she had.

"Mabel was perfectly free to go if she wanted. I even offered to pay the extra charge. But she was afraid of catching one of her deep colds sleeping out on the ground."

"You mean she betrayed me!"

"I don't know what you mean by that. She was delighted to have an excuse to get out of it. You're plenty old enough to face the fact that many of the women of your father's family are chronically timid. I wouldn't mind it, except for the fact that they put up such a constant front of being spunkier than I am. Aunt Mabel has a dread of infection or of being physically hurt. That's one of the reasons I've encouraged her to become a nurse. I think it ought to help her."

Mother was inclined, as I grew older, to become franker with me about Father's family, of whom, she used to claim, he was the single star. I suppose she was trying to warn me about possible inherited characteristics.

"But you're timid yourself," I protested, in defense of the paternal blood. "You can't deny that you were timid about everything at the ranch, can you?"

"I was timid for you and your father, yes. Not for myself. I shouldn't in the least have minded taking any sort of pack trip."

It was obvious that she judged herself differently from Father's female relatives, who were afraid for themselves. And over the next years I came reluctantly to agree with her. There *was* something disappointing about the Ruggles women, even Aunt Mabel. The men (Father always excepted) were different. Grandpa and Uncle Jonathan never disappointed me because I never expected anything from them. But poor Aunt Mabel, with all her cheer and warmth and sympathy, seemed to promise the moon. And she never quite delivered it.

After Aunt Mabel had graduated from the Bellevue Nurses School, in the first third of her class, she took a job at New York Hospital, where she was soon promoted to be head nurse of her floor. All the family were proud of her, but it sometimes seemed to my perhaps oversensitive ears that there was a faint note of the old condescension in the very clamor of their approval. I thought I could make out the message "No, no, we don't share any of the stuffiness of the silly old past. We think it's just as important to be a nurse as to be a wife or mother or even a stockbroker. And anyway Aunt Mabel has shown she has all the Ruggles guts and spirit. God bless you, Aunt Mabel!"

But no sooner was Aunt Mabel launched on her career than events seemed to conspire to get her out of it. Grandmother was partially paralyzed by a stroke, and Grandpa's fretful and near senile fussing over her made it almost impossible for nurses to perform their tasks. Only Aunt Mabel could control him, and she had to take more and more time off to manage things at home, finally quitting her job altogether to care for her parents full time. I had hoped that Grandmother's death would bring her release, but as Grandpa was now utterly senile and Uncle Jonathan no help to anybody, Aunt Mabel seemed permanently trapped. Again I was disgusted by the family's acceptance of her sacrifice, and told her so, but she shook her head and said she was only doing what she had to do and that it didn't help to make a fuss. As the Great Depression was then at its worst and even nurses were out of jobs, I reluctantly shut my mouth.

My parents weathered those dark years fairly well, as Father's law firm was able to make money out of corporate dissolutions and reorganizations as well as bankruptcies, but Grandpa's securities, mismanaged by Uncle Jonathan, who persisted in seeing permanent recovery in every slightest upturn of the market, dropped to a quarter of their 1929 values. This disaster was compounded by Uncle Jonathan's refusal, despite Father's objections, to make any reduction in the Ruggles scale of living, with the result that Grandpa's children's inheritance was mostly lost. I remember Mother's dry comment, when Uncle Jonathan at last consented to put the Bar Harbor house on the market, but without telling anyone, that the whole thing was "too *Cherry Orchard* to be believed." And Uncle Jonathan's removal, with Grandpa and Aunt Mabel, to a Park Avenue apartment, ostensibly to save the greater expense of running a town house, proved a pathetically inadequate remedy.

Aunt Mabel paid the greatest ultimate price for this

foolishness. While cheerfully proclaiming her readiness to adapt herself to a new and perhaps a braver world, and valiantly recognizing that one couldn't "drink champagne on a beer income," she still betrayed, in the way she sneered at a "stuffy" past that was so much grander than her present, a certain resentment that she should have been brought up to expect a different way of life.

When Grandpa died at last, aged ninety, Aunt Mabel moved to a two-room flat and went back to work in the hospital, but she was almost sixty now, and she felt out of touch and overworked. She soon retired as a nurse and took a part-time job fund raising for her old settlement house, where she was much loved and poorly paid. Her standards were always high. If she took a block of seats for a theater benefit, and the play closed before the scheduled night, she would not, as most charities did, write to the subscribers in the hope they would not want their money back; she would send the refund checks right out.

More and more now she was called on to visit members of her aging family when they took ill. She spent weeks at a time with Aunt Ellen Clark, whose husband was dying by inches of emphysema, and with my parents, after Father's first heart attack. She never received any remuneration for this, only occasionally what Mother and Aunt Ellen called "handsome presents." I think they really believed, at least when they were in their country places, that it was a vacation for Aunt Mabel to "get out of the city." I recalled bitterly Grandmother's plea against "house visits." Evidently these were only permitted a "lady" if rendered without charge.

Aunt Mabel's last family nursing job, for she survived him by less than a year, was with Uncle Jonathan. He was living in an apartment hotel, from which, even after the diagnosis of his terminal cancer, Aunt Mabel insisted that he not be moved.

"In a hospital they'll just keep him alive for months," she told my parents. "I've had all I need of that. I'll take care of him and see that he has an easy end. I've set up a daybed in his little dressing room. You, Lina, can relieve me, if you like, for a couple of hours in the afternoon, and Ellen can spell me on an occasional weekend. You'll see. It will work out fine."

My most vivid memory of what she went through was on the last visit I paid to Uncle Jonathan. His mind must have been affected by the heavy drugs he was receiving, for although as stentorianly articulate as ever, he was hardly rational. He sat up stiffly in his bed, clad in a splendid red velvet robe, shaved and combed and immaculate, an unwrinkled sheet over his nether regions, no book, magazine, or even radio in sight, apparently resigned to his state of dignified atrophy. He greeted me with his customary cordiality. It made little difference that now he had no idea who I was.

"Very good of you to pay me this visit, young fellow. In a few days I should be as good as new. But so long as you're here, there is one thing you could do for me."

"Certainly, sir."

"If you could just step into the manager's office on your way out, and tell him that woman — I can hardly call her a lady — has been using my bathroom again."

I wondered if he meant Aunt Mabel whom I could see, reading a magazine, through the half-open door to the dressing room. But she raised her head and winked at me.

"Does she often use it?"

"She's in there right now! Sitting on my john, if you please, naked as a jaybird. Don't you find that outrageous in a supposedly first-class hotel? And charging me what they charge?"

I followed his indignant glare to the closed bathroom door. "You say she's in there *now?*"

"Well, go see for yourself, if you don't believe me!"

I think I was really about to, so convincing was his lunacy, when Aunt Mabel rose and came in to open the bathroom door.

"I've told you once, and I don't want to have to tell you again," she called into the unseen interior, "that you're not to use Mr. Ruggles's bathroom. Now scat! Put a towel around you, and leave by the corridor door. I won't have you traipsing through Mr. Ruggles's room and putting us all to shame." She paused for a moment, as if seeing that her order was executed, and then closed the bathroom door. "It's all right, Jonathan. I don't think she'll come back this time."

When I told Mother about this, she said she had been through the same scene. "I wonder what episode it awakens in his murky past. I guess it's just as well we don't know."

"It makes me sick to think of Aunt Mabel's brave career ending up chasing imagined nudes out of Uncle Jonathan's loo."

"But isn't that what nursing's all about?"

"Perhaps. But with the dignity of a regular job, a uniform, a ward, a constant change of patients. Not just being the unpaid kid sister of a querulous old bachelor who never gave a damn about her or anyone else."

"You're getting too old, Daniel, to be so judgmental. Can't you see that your aunt Mabel has succeeded at last in 'owning' all the people who used to seem so superior to her? That is, the people *she* chose to think were superior? I mean your grandparents and Uncle Jonathan. And even, to a lesser extent, your father and Aunt Ellen. Mabel's had them all, in her own fashion, one after the other."

"You mean she's a kind of moral vulture? That she waits for the final illness and then moves in to feed her hungry soul?"

"My child, you're being ridiculous. I simply mean that she's found what she considers her ultimate utility."

"Because her family had broken her on the wheel? Because that's all she had left to expect?"

"How many people can achieve what they want in life?"

"And that's all you think life has to offer? How can you so downgrade it?"

"Because I'm not as greedy as you are."

When Aunt Mabel died the following year, I was very

much distressed, as the executor named in her will, that I was unable to find the biblical quotation she had wanted inscribed on her tombstone. She had told me it was in a drawer of her desk, but it wasn't, and I ransacked her little apartment in vain. Mother thought I was making too much of it.

"She probably threw it out with some junk mail. She was always doing things like that. What difference does it really make?"

"It was her last wish, Mother!"

"Then she should have been more careful about it. Anyway, she can't care now."

"But what shall I put on the stone?"

"Won't 'I know that my redeemer liveth' do?"

And indeed I couldn't think of anything better. Mother had a way of having the last word.

Uncle Theo

UNCLE THEODORE FISHER, twelve years younger than my mother, had not been what is sometimes called an "afterthought" of my maternal grandparents, much less a "mistake," but rather the happy conclusion of a sad domestic period in their lives that had seen three miscarriages and a stillborn child. Mother had just about resigned herself to being an only child when this surviving little bundle arrived, and she at once endowed it with all the misty affection of which an excitable and romantic young girl is capable. Uncle Theo found himself at a tender age the object of near idolatry by his parents and only sibling. He was at all times a perfect gentleman about it.

My grandfather Fisher died of cancer when Uncle Theo was only thirteen, shortly after my mother and father were married, and my desolated and lonely grandmother, though reputedly a woman of strong character, could not bear to send her "baby" off to boarding school with the rest of his friends, but kept him with her in New

York at Browning, a day school that had grades up to college. I believe that she thus saddled her son with a sense
of inferiority to boys who had experienced what he probably considered the rough-and-tumble of boarding schools,
making him, with the added factor of his slender build,
inclined to be envious of the athletes he met when he
went to Yale. It must have always seemed to him that he
had something to make up for. He was determined to row
and play football, and in the summer to ride and play
tennis, as well as the best, even if he was always hurting
himself by trying too hard, wrenching his back in a scrim-
mage or breaking an ankle in a fall from too high a jump,
but always going back for more.

Everyone liked him. He was modest but not humble,
with handsome features and large sympathetic brown
eyes, an even temper and quiet good manners that con-
trasted with his sister's more emphatic ones. In 1916,
impatient at his country's continued neutrality, he went
to Canada to enlist in the air force, showing an unexpected firmness of character in refusing to listen to the
desperate objections of a mother commonly supposed to
dominate him. It was unfortunate that, afflicted with the
same dread disease that had killed her husband, she
should have died while her son was overseas, leaving him
perhaps with the uncomfortable notion that his "heroism"
might have hastened her end. But if he had such misgiv-
ings, he never voiced them. It was one of his principles
never to be what he called "soppy."

Returning from France after the war, decorated but

whole, he lived for a time with us. He and Mother had inherited the Fisher brownstone on West Forty-ninth Street, and she and Father were scrupulous in allotting him a whole floor to himself and his due share of care from the four maids, but he must have still felt occasionally a bit pushed to the wall by their noisy young family. If he did, again he never said so. He was always considerate and charming. My brother, Jasper, and I were delighted at the attentive and flattering adult interest that he took in our games and confidences, and the maids adored him, fiercely enjoining a strict silence upon us on mornings when he happened to be sleeping late. He and Father were always on the most friendly terms, and I suspect that the latter had occasional need of his young brother-in-law in dealing with Mother's anxieties and alarms over her sons' habits and health. For Uncle Theo, for whose welfare she had felt, particularly after their mother's demise, a quasimaternal concern, had, by the gentleness of his nature and the persistence of his sunny common sense, succeeded in moderating some of her more inordinate worries. It was not that Mother bowed to her brother's opinions, for apprehensiveness was too much her master to allow her to bow to anyone's, but at least she listened to him. She even listened when he half banteringly (but only half) charged her with the sin of soppiness.

They formed a curious contrast, these two, so much and so little alike. Both were quick, bright, and intensely loyal persons. Both had the high moral standards of the well-bred agnostic. And they laughed at the same things.

But while Mother was rather steamily domestic, putting too heavy an emphasis on the value of what to her were the "real" things of life — children and conjugal love and family empathy — Uncle Theo showed a distinct respect for the standards of the "great world." This was manifest in his careful and colorful dressing, his fondness for clubs and parties and his cultivation of what his exact contemporary, Scott Fitzgerald, called the "beautiful people." To Uncle Theo the term "gentleman," uniting as it did for him an always neat and polished exterior with an equally neat and polished inner integrity, was a constant guide. And I think he always believed that Mother had misconceived her role, which was less to be an earth mother than a lady of the world. He may well have been right.

Although he took a job as a customer's man in a well-known brokerage house, he allowed one to infer that this was only temporary. He was distinctly impatient with the limitations of his urban existence. In retrospect I can see that he was really more impatient with the limitations of his urban income. Uncle Theo had inherited enough money to be what the rich called "comfortable," but that was not his idea of the good life. Not for him was the Tudor house on Long Island, the bridge-playing Junior League wife, the country club, the two cars (one a station wagon), and the three children (two boys and a girl). No, his mind wandered to climes where a man could play polo and even run a small racing stable on the income required for those suburban niceties. If he was never soppy, he was nonetheless always romantic. I have mentioned

Scott Fitzgerald. His was really more the world of Somerset Maugham.

He found his ultimate solution in South America. He boldly invested the bulk of his capital in a cattle ranch in the Argentine and disappeared from Forty-ninth Street. Mother was appalled. She predicted financial ruin and an early return to his floor in the family brownstone, but her crystal ball was clouded. Uncle Theo not only remained in Argentina, he prospered there. His long and entertaining letters to Mother, always read aloud to the family, showed him moving happily in the horsy circles he so ardently admired, and they were copiously illustrated with snapshots showing him astride a favorite mount, in a polo cap equipped for a match, or under a wide-brimmed straw hat ready to round up steers. He seemed to have proved that some dreams at least could be realized.

Nor was there any disillusionment on his first long visit home, to seek additional bank financing for his ranch. He stayed with us in his old rooms and seemed to have plenty of time to accompany me on afternoon visits to a store that specialized in wooden animals, cleverly carved and painted, with limbs that moved, which I had been slowly purchasing, one by one, with my carefully hoarded allowance. Uncle Theo threw my collection deliriously out of balance by adding to it some of the larger animals that I had not been able to afford, and at the end of his visit he crowned my menagerie with the beast I had only dreamed of acquiring, the great black Indian elephant with the howdah and detachable mahout. When I told him ecstatically that I had never imagined that I should own such a treasure, he became briefly serious.

"Remember, Dan, there's nothing in the whole wide world you can't have. You only have to want it enough. And be determined enough to get it."

The idea fascinated me, but when I asked Mother about it, after Uncle Theo had gone back to South America, she seemed more amused than impressed.

"Do you suppose he meant what Jesus said in the Bible, 'Ask and ye shall receive'?" I put to her.

"No, I don't think he meant that at all. I think Uncle Theo's wants are more of the earth — earthy." And she turned to my father and added in that tone reserved for purely adult communications, "I hope he didn't mean Mrs. Leach."

That was the first time I heard the name of the lady who was to become, five years later, my Aunt Laura. She was not discussed further in my presence, but it was clear that she was very much disapproved and was somehow the reason for Uncle Theo's continued (and equally disapproved) bachelor state. It was not until I had been sent to Chelton School in Massachusetts and learned the facts (or fantasies) of life that I was able to put together, with the aid of my more sophisticated friends, the explanation that my uncle was "entangled" in an affair with a married woman who could not obtain her "freedom." It was the one touch needed to promote Uncle Theo to the rank of the ultimately romantic.

·   ·   ·

A change in whatever his long-term extramarital situation had been occurred when I was sixteen, and now Mother wrote to me quite openly about it. Mrs. Leach's freedom, however scandalously obtained, appeared to be in the offing, and she was coming north with Uncle Theo to establish the six-week residence required in Nevada for her divorce, after which he would presumably enjoy the honor of becoming her third husband. But the really electric news contained in Mother's letter was that they would first spend a week in Concord with Mrs. Leach's sister and drive over to Chelton to take me out for a Saturday lunch.

I was then a fifth-former and had long emerged from the shadows of my first two years at the school. Indeed I now regarded myself as a kind of butterfly that had escaped its drab cocoon to adorn the academic garden. My marks had soared; my stories had appeared in the *Cheltonian;* I had had a modest part in the annual school play. Of course none of this added up to anything like the popularity of an athlete or school prefect, but I had developed a small circle of congenial friends who liked privately to sneer at the "philistine" stars of the playing fields. It was also, even less attractively, a group that tended to admire worldly things. We noted the swell cars of visiting families, the Hispanos and Isottas; we relished the occasional stepfather with a European title, and I'm afraid we even found the divorced parents more glamorous than the stodgily faithful. I was enchanted at the prospect of showing off my young uncle and the mysterious Argentine to whom he was connected by no legal link.

Of course, I knew that she was not Argentine at all and that she was a good dozen years older than Uncle Theo. Mother had carefully filled in the details. She had been born a New Yorker (she had actually been a class ahead of Mother at the Brearley School) and had married first an Argentine and then an Englishman stationed in the embassy in Buenos Aires. The first marriage had ended in divorce; the second was now ending in scandal.

And she was certainly, at fifty-plus, no longer a beauty, though one could see she must have once been pretty. This I made out when they drove up that Saturday and parked outside my dormitory. Uncle Theo leaped from the car and helped Mrs. Leach out with a gallantry of which I took immediate note, for he did not even greet me until she did. Had there been a puddle before her I think he would have flung his coat across it.

"So this is young Dan. How I recognize the Fisher eyes! Will you be a polo player too, Dan?"

Her voice was high-pitched and musical, her lips scarlet and beautifully shaped. Her face was round, but the features were fine and the appraising eyes just faintly mocking. She wore a mink coat to which was pinned an orchid corsage. Her hair, tightly set, was a dyed auburn, and her figure might have been called verging on the plump, though Mother had used the dreadful word "dumpy." But then Mother would. I could see that Mrs. Leach belonged to that world of stylish women who made no bones about finding Mother's standards "frumpish," a world, oddly enough — for everything is relative — that

Father's sisters were inclined to accuse Mother herself of belonging to.

Uncle Theo now asked me if we could take a turn around the Lawn, the grass circle on which Chelton's red-brick, white-colonnaded buildings bordered. "No Cook's tour, mind you, Dan," he added with a wink. "Laura is like one of those paleontologists who can reconstruct the skeleton of a dinosaur from the bone of one toe. A very little goes a long way with her."

"Now, Theodore, I won't have you make me out one of those silly, easily bored women. Shush!" She gave his wrist a small tap, but not a coy one. It was immediately evident that she was used to control, a situation hardly surprising to one brought up in a family such as mine. "I want Dan to show me everything that he thinks may interest me."

Mrs. Leach had the quick, appraising eye that minimizes the number of steps that need be taken to view sufficiently any landmark, a characteristic, I later learned, of expatriates with long practice in guiding their visiting countrymen through historical sites. She showed more interest in pictures and inscriptions than in classrooms or playing fields; she perused a few of the memorial plaques in the chapel and paused to take in the principal portraits in the dining hall. Her comments revealed that she viewed Chelton with considerable approval, but more as the caste product of old Boston and New York families than as a church school founded on a devout Episcopal faith. I smiled to myself to think how indignantly our headmaster, Dr. Minturn, would have rejected her endorsement.

"Duncan Saunders! — I haven't thought of him in ages. — Oh, of course, he died in the Argonne. — He was engaged to Charlotte Saltonstall. — I wonder how that would have worked out. — Better than what she got, I daresay. — And Jerry Lascelles. — He had polio. — Poor boy, how girls used to scare him! — I always wondered if he wasn't a bit queer. — Ah, look at Mrs. Minturn! — You can see right away she was a Lowell. — It's a Sargent, isn't it? — No? Ellen Emmet Rand? — Oh, well, she was the poor man's Sargent. — It took Boston's best to make a finishing school for all you horrid little Manhattan boys, didn't it? — My, my, look at that list of names. — Not a single Jewish one. — Isn't that just a touch provincial?"

I had been wondering how I should be able to tell when she had had enough. I needn't have worried. She was perfectly definite about it. After a forty-minute stroll she turned to Uncle Theo. "I'm afraid this little girl is getting rather thirsty. Where did you make that reservation for lunch?"

We went to an inn in the local village where Uncle Theo had reserved a table in an alcove. He ordered "setups" for himself and his friend and filled the glasses from a silver flask extracted from his overcoat pocket. Prohibition had recently ceased, but it was still not common for guests at country inns to drink at their meals. Uncle Theo's experience, however, in Latin climes had equipped him to deal tactfully and firmly with the stiffest proprietors.

Of course, he knew too much about boarding schools to offer me a drink, but I noted that Mrs. Leach consumed two large whiskeys before she even glanced at the menu and had a third with her lunch. I felt very cosmopolitan.

"I have a favor to ask of you, Dan," she said, after she had merely toyed with the soufflé that I had eaten with a few bites. "I want you to act as my legate to your parents. I'm sure that they frown on divorce, do they not? And if they frown on one, they must really shake their gory locks at two."

Uncle Theo was obviously taken by surprise. "Laura, my dear, must we get into this?"

"Yes, Theodore, we must. Is there any reason I shouldn't be absolutely frank with your nephew?" She eyed him sharply a moment. "Well, *is* there?"

"I suppose not, my dear."

"Very well, then. Your uncle and I, Dan, plan to be married just as soon as my decree is final. My last husband sued me for divorce in the Argentine, as I have no doubt your mother has told you."

"Please, Laura! Is this really necessary?"

"Theodore, if you keep interrupting me, we'll never get through." A second stare subdued him. "My husband, as I was saying, started out by being thoroughly nasty. He based his suit on my friendship with your uncle. Since then his lawyer and mine have gotten together, and he has agreed, after certain considerations, including, I'm afraid, some financial ones in which your uncle has been very generous (more so than I would have been), to withdraw his action. He will now file what the lawyers call 'an appearance and consent' in my Nevada suit against *him*. Except I shall be a lady and not say horrid things about him. Only that he trumped my ace in a bridge game or any peccadillo that will satisfy that very civilized state." Here Mrs. Leach threw back her head and gave vent to a high, rather shrill laugh of a surprising silliness. I say surprising because it did not seem to fit with her air of considerable dignity. It was a humorless laugh, even a defiant one, as if the world she had to cope with was really too idiotic to be funny. "In short, the whole dragged-out matter will at last be settled amicably as it should have been in the beginning. What is the point of adding more hate to a world that is already as full of it as the most ardent moralist could wish?"

"None, I'm sure," I agreed, proud to be consulted.

"And if, then, everything has been arranged to the satisfaction of the three parties most concerned, is there any real reason for others to object?" Here she glanced inquiringly around the room as if she had been addressing the other tables.

"No reason at all."

"I'm glad you agree with me. I can see that you're an intelligent young man. And if you can see the issues so clearly, don't you think you might persuade your mother to?"

"I can certainly try." Mother, Father, Chelton, Dr. Minturn, and the Ten Commandments went down the drain. I would have sacrificed anything to appear a man of the world to Mrs. Leach.

"Well, there's no immediate hurry about it, as we shall be in Reno for six weeks. What a fate! However, I suppose I shall be able to indulge in a bit of gambling, and your uncle can go riding in the desert. When we next meet we'll be aunt and nephew!"

"Aunt Laura! May I call you that now?"

"No. For you I shall be simply Laura."

After lunch my new relative went upstairs to rest in a bedroom that Uncle Theo had had the foresight to engage, and he and I went for a little walk in the pretty village. I asked him how he and "Laura" had met. (How proud I was to use her Christian name! My family was very formal in intergenerational relations.) He at once waxed enthusiastically reminiscent.

"It happened just like that!" He snapped his fingers and then gazed reflectively at the vista of fields between two cottages. "As all the best things in life do. I was at the races, standing up near the start, and I happened to turn, just after they were off, and saw her get up and move to the front of her box. She was all in white, with a wide-brimmed straw hat, and she was holding up her binoculars to follow the race. I remember she had on long white gloves, too. I didn't watch that race, only her. And I saw her turn when it was over, and her horse had won, and cast the most radiant smile you ever saw at the lucky guys in the row behind her."

To me it was like one of the wonderful movies of the period. I could imagine a first shot of Greta Garbo, turning to flash her enchanting eyes on the stylishly garbed gentlemen in her box, while Clark Gable looked feverishly on. Of course, I could see that Mrs. Leach was too mature and plump to be Garbo and Uncle Theo too slight and slender to be Gable, but I was already enough of a writer to envisage different worlds as seen through different eyes and to suspect that romance may be largely in the heart of the romantic.

Uncle Theo must have suspected that his beloved would not be seen by all in so glowing a light, for he proceeded to emphasize that to appreciate her rare quality one had to see her in her adopted environment. In the Argentine, on a verandah overlooking wide fields of grazing cattle, dispensing drinks to handsome, jesting Latins, her high laugh ringing out above the gallant chatter, Laura Leach was something more than a visiting relative peering at plaques in the Chelton chapel. And how could she show her steel in a New England boarding school? For steel, it appeared, she had, too, as well as charm. Riding out alone on her first husband's ranch she had once encountered a couple of horse thieves and chased them off the land brandishing a small pearl-handled pistol!

Mother, however, proved quite insensitive to Laura's romantic appeal when I next came home and made my abortive effort to convince her of it.

"I see she took you in easily enough. Really, Dan, you must learn not to be such a pushover. Or else, in a few years' time you'll be bringing home some stout old rumpot and telling me she's Helen of Troy. But what I really can't put up with is the idea of Laura Leach conspiring with you, as if you were two youngsters, to get around an old hag of convention like me. Why, I was still wearing bloomers at school when she was already in her first long dress!"

I was so taken aback by this cattiness on Mother's part that I decided to abandon, at least with her, my advocacy of Mrs. Leach's cause. And indeed it was not a case that could possibly be won before that tribunal. Mother had to be left to face her brother's imminent marriage in her own fashion. And when the telegram came with the news of their union, she did indeed respond with the appearance of generosity. She went at once to the little safe in the dressing alcove of her bedroom and took out the big diamond brooch that had belonged to her mother and which was certainly the most valuable piece of jewelry that she owned. It was the puritan in her that obliged her to give to the sister-in-law she detested her finest possession. But I was horrified to hear her mutter, as she took it out of its case and unclasped the long pin, "I hope she sticks it through her jugular vein!"

Now such savagery was not characteristic of Mother. But she felt that her brother's very soul was at stake. It was not simply that Aunt Laura was older and bibulous and that their union extinguished all hope of the family on which Mother placed so weighty an emphasis; it was that her sister-in-law purported to justify all the values that she felt were cheapest in her brother's assessment of life.

It was unfortunate that a cocktail party should have

been the entertainment that my parents offered the bridal couple when they came east after a brief honeymoon in Palm Springs. Some hundred or more of our friends and relations gathered on the second floor, the *piano nobile* as we used jokingly to call it, of the family brownstone to greet the effervescent bride, blinking and smiling over her orchid corsage, emitting her high, shrill laugh, higher and shriller with each of her constantly replenished glasses.

Why did she drink so much that evening? Why did she have to subside at last in a suddenly silent bundle on a sofa and then be assisted from the room by a solicitous husband past the clumps of pretending-not-to-be-watching guests? Such scenes, I gathered later, were not typical of her life in South America. There, if she was always drinking, she was never drunk. And it could not have been nervousness at the presence of the assembled tribe, for they could not have been more formidable than horse thieves. No, I believe she did what she did that evening to humiliate her hostess. And if so, she certainly succeeded, for I have never seen Mother weep such angry and passionate tears as she did when that party was over. Yet was the success all Laura's? Surely there must have been some fierce inner spark of satisfaction in Mother's heart in seeing her brother's wife turn herself before his eyes — and before the world, too — into just the picture that she had held up so warningly before him. Surely, even in the desolation of being proved right, there had to have been some hint of compensation in the triumph of one's own perspicacity.

Or was Uncle Theo simply forgotten by both women in the indulgence of their mutual hatred? Did puritan and sybarite have eyes for any but each other as they unsheathed their swords? Woe to the peacemaker who dared come between them! If Mother seemed momentarily to triumph over the wilted figure of Aunt Laura, her eyes half closed, settled on that sofa and listing with crumpled orchids to one side, did the latter not fell with a Parthian dart the hostess made to look as if she were giving just the kind of party she most deplored and showing the sacred Fisher family in a light not usually focused on it?

But if there was a winner in the unseemly struggle it was Uncle Theo. I don't think anyone present would soon forget the dignity with which he approached the seated Laura and, leaning down, murmured, "I think, my dear, it may be time we were getting back to the St. Regis." And he actually glanced at his watch as if their departure were dictated by nothing but their schedule. "We've had a long day, and I've ordered supper sent up at eight." And then he reached down to take her by the elbows and propel her slowly but surely to her feet. "Careful there," he cautioned her in a tone as natural as if she were merely suffering from some mild chronic ailment of which all were sympathetically aware. "Dan will take your other arm." Which I instantly did. And so we got her down the stairs and into a taxi.

"Thanks, old boy," he said with the same easy manner as I closed the door. "Be sure you lunch with us before we leave for B.A. Laura loves talking to you. It was a nice party, wasn't it?" And he turned to give the driver the address.

Was it acting? Does the perfect gentleman ever have to act? I think that he believed that his wife was so splendid a being and that this was so generally recognized (with the exception of Mother, and didn't everyone know about older sisters?) that her little lapses would be as easily overlooked as a small crack on the smooth marble surface of an idol. Was anyone faultless? Didn't Cleopatra have a vile temper and Mary Stuart bad judgment?

Uncle Theo had got what he wanted, and he was perfectly content with his bargain. During the war, when he joined the OSS and was overseas for a year and a half, he always afterward described his sacrifice in the struggle against the Axis powers as "eighteen months of Laura." Until her death of a liver ailment, ten years after their marriage, he remained happily proud of her. He had married romance and he was faithful to it.

Two years after Laura's death he and I took a short motor trip in France. He was very much his old quiet, courteous self, but there was a subdued quality to his enthusiasm, a touch of effort in his facing of each new town or castle that seemed to bespeak his desire to be home on the ranch that he associated with the deceased. I was sure he would never marry again. But he was not despondent; he still had some faith in the future. One night at dinner I asked him if he still believed that one could get anything in life that one really wanted.

"Oh, yes!" And he was suddenly grave. "Look at me. I got Laura. It took me six years but I got her."

I as gravely acquiesced. "And are there still things you want?"

"Not as much, of course. But yes, there are still things."

"Such as?"

"Well . . ." He paused to reflect, or perhaps to decide if I was worthy of the confidence. Then he clenched a fist. "I'll tell you, Dan." And when he did it was without any hint of apprehension that I might find his eagerness undue. "Life isn't over yet. I may *still* become secretary of the Jockey Club!"

Leonard Armster

IT WAS NOT until a year before Leonard Armster's suicide, at the age of twenty-four, an event that had shocked
and horrified all the friends who had seen in him an important future writer or journalist or politician — certainly
an important something — that I discovered what I still,
more than four decades later, believe to have been the
clue to his disordered personality. And even then I never
suspected that it would lead to so fatal a consequence. On
the contrary, just before his death Len had seemed fairly
launched on the brilliant career so many had anticipated
for him. He was a reporter for *Globe*, and good rumor
had it that he was to be sent abroad as a war correspondent. Had he gone he might have made his name covering the battle of Britain.

I am not going to give the clue here, as the reader, detached from the situation, may pick it up more rapidly
than I did. People differed drastically about Len, some
liking him immediately and some detesting him, but there

seemed a consensus that his imagination was too vivid
and his ambition too violent for him to be wholly trust-
worthy. Most of our classmates at Yale, at least the prep
school crowd, saw him as an entertaining and subtle social
climber whose wit and easy adaptability with people
made up in goodly measure for any deficiency in moral
character, if deficiency there were. For we still talked
about moral character in those days. There was little consensus, however, as to the goal of his climbing. It sometimes seemed that any altitude (other than in athletics at
which he was always hopeless) existed only for him to
scale. If there was a peak around, the phrase might have
been, Len wanted to sit on it. But never alone. One thing
at least was definite about him; he was insatiably, incur-
ably gregarious.

Some might have deemed it a grave disadvantage that
he had neither good looks nor any great charm. He had a
tall, rather spindly figure and a poor complexion somewhat redeemed by fine brown eyes and thick black curly
hair; his laugh was high and rasping, and his manner
either a little too bold or a little too obsequious. Yet he
managed to attract the most unlikely types — football
players, do-gooders (or what we used to call "Christers"),
and the rich, white-shoe (for they wore them) fraternity
crowd — by the sheer power of his intellect, characterized,
at least in his social life, by a remarkable, an occasionally
alarming capability of penetrating the deepest personality
secrets of those whom he chose to cultivate. Sometimes
this skill of discovery amused the persons subject to his

probing; sometimes it flattered them; sometimes it frightened them. But in all cases it proved useful to Len.

His social background was no more help to him than his appearance. He was the only child of a divorced couple of small means. His father, an insurance salesman, lived with a flashy but fading blonde in Brooklyn and paid small heed to Len or the bills of his education; his mother, whose home in Newburgh he shared, a dreary, horse-faced woman, supported herself as best she could as a broker for small real estate deals. But Len's genius encompassed the garnering of more scholarships and paying prizes than one would have thought possible, including two years at Andover Academy. He dressed well and never borrowed except from close friends, and he was always ready to pick up the check when it was his turn. It took me some time to detect the shrewd, vigilant planning that had to underlie his seeming casualness about money.

I shared the general view of his character when, in the middle of our sophomore year, he turned his roving attention in my direction and began to drop in to my room in Davenport an evening or so a week. We both used to go on Sunday evenings to Professor Samuel Hemenway's in Berkeley, where a group of Shakespeare enthusiasts read the plays aloud, and this formed the pleasant topic of our initial chats. But we soon went on to less intellectual themes. I knew exactly what social goals Len was after, but this amused rather than irritated me. I was even willing to let him use me, for such advantages as I could offer him. I was certainly not one of the leaders of the class, but I knew them all. My family had an ample apartment in New York and a country place on Long Island, in both of which a visitor could be comfortably put up. And I went to a good number of debutante parties, in the city and on the North Shore, to which a house guest could easily be taken. A stronger personality than mine would have been harder for Len to manipulate; a weaker would not have been able to push him into all the places where he wanted to be pushed. Oh, he had it figured out!

Now I realize that I have just made him sound odious. But he wasn't. He wasn't at all. In the first place there was no question of deception. He knew at all times that I knew what he was up to. You might put it that between us there existed a kind of symbiosis. I was to give him a leg up socially, and he was to introduce me to an intellectual world of thought that I had not known. We were writing for the *Yale Literary Magazine,* and I had begun (very daringly) to wonder if there might be a future in letters for me. I had been raised in a commercial society where the arts played a role strictly confined to entertainment. Pictures, plays, novels, and music were "all right," but they could never be "real," that is, a fitting occupation for a man, unless he was "great." In other words, in the eyes of my parents and their friends, I couldn't be a writer unless I were John Galsworthy (whose stock was then very high). They did not admit to a middle class in literature. Len cleared all this away for me. To him writers, artists, and even actors were quite as important as lawyers or doctors. He made no distinction between the success of a popular playwright and that of a great banker. He broadened my perspective to cover just about everything a man might want to do. And he had a low opinion of Galsworthy.

Also, most important of all, with his quick understanding, his wit and congeniality, he could be wonderful company. Nor was he cold, as might have been expected from what I have said of his habitual calculations. On the contrary, his nature was highly emotional, even at times frankly sentimental. If he directed the flow of his affections toward persons selected more by the mind than the heart, that did not mean that the heart did not follow. Len liked me, and I liked him. It was as if he had winked and said: "Take me where I want to go, and I'll make it worth your while." But we were both too sensible ever to articulate the bargain. Some things are better left unsaid.

We began to do things together. We went a lot to the movies, a richer field in the mid-1930s than today; we dined at Mory's; more often, of an evening, we would drink and talk. We never studied together because Len never seemed to study; I think he must have prepared for each class a mere half hour before, depending on the rapid speed of his reading and the inexhaustible depth of his memory. In our talks he soon learned everything there was to be learned about me: my opinions and ambitions, my family, my childhood, my early unhappy boarding school days, and my later happier ones, while I learned really very little about him. Yet our talks never seemed one-sided. He had a curious way of inserting himself so solidly into my life that he seemed to be exercising a kind of domination over my existence even in the years before I knew him.

His voice comes back to me now, making gleeful fun of my vanity in the moment of my breakthrough at boarding school from the leprosy of unpopularity to the fragile eminence of finally obtained high grades. He brought, as he frequently did, the duc de Saint-Simon to his aid. I think Len always intended one day to do for his world what the diarist duke had done for Versailles. Certainly, he knew whole pages by heart.

"So you actually rose in two years' time from the black pit to the celestial regions? Oh, in grades, of course, I know, only in grades. I quite understand the qualification. Grades at Andover, also, were not the mark of a 'real' success. But we benighted souls must make do with what we have, mustn't we? And I can see you, sitting in the smugness of sheer ecstasy as the veteran headmaster solemnly reads out the monthly grades to the assembled student body, knowing that when he comes to yours, there will be mandatory applause, as for every boy whose average is over ninety. Mandatory? Who cares, so long as one's ears are thrilled with the contact of palm on palm! Oh, bliss ineffable! How your heart must have pounded! How it must have made up for the hazing, the sitting on benches in games, the never being called. Like the little duke, after the demise of the Sun King, when he sat in Parlement to witness the downgrading of the royal bastards below the dukes." Here Len's voice rose to a kind of croon as he broke into quotation. " 'I truly felt as though I were going to swoon, for my heart seemed to swell within me and could find no room in which to expand. I remembered the long days and years of servitude, those unhappy times when, like a victim, I was dragged to the Parlement to witness the triumph of the bastards, as they rose by degrees to a pinnacle above our heads. Then I thought of this day of law and justice, this dreadful retribution which had elevated us by the force of recoil. I could rightly congratulate myself that all this had been brought about by me. I triumphed, I was avenged, I rejoiced in my vengeance. I delighted in the satisfaction of my strongest, most eager and most steadfast desires!' "

Len was soon a visitor on weekends in New York. He made a great and successful effort with Mother, although she was at first distrustful of him. She could not help but be intrigued by a young man who took such an intelligent interest in her world, including the New York of her childhood and the charitable activities in which she took so much part. He got her talking about her friends and relations, rather too much. "He makes indiscretion seem like intellectual honesty," she admitted ruefully once. Len saw at once that she was the more dynamic of my parents, and he tended to downgrade Father, though always treating him with marked good manners. He underestimated Father, who sensed the perfunctory quality of Len's questions to him about "downtown" and disliked him.

June came, and with it the season of Long Island debutante parties. Marquees were raised on the lawns of estates along the North Shore, and long tables with white linen and wineglasses awaited the hundreds of young men and women, interested only in one another, on whom this vast expenditure was largely wasted. Len came down to visit us for a week in the course of which I was to take him to no fewer than five big parties.

Before the events of our first gala evening, which were to embrace two of them, Len and I sat in our tuxedos on the terrace of my family's house, sipping a preliminary cocktail. Rather enjoying myself, for I was for once on ground that I knew better than he, I proceeded to give him what I deemed some needed instruction.

"Tonight we have a dinner followed by a supper dance. That means that we each have a minimum of four duty dances."

Len, aping the demeanor of a patient child, spread the fingers of his left hand and held up the index of his right, ready to count.

"First?"

"First, the girl giving the dinner. Then the girl honored at the dance. Then the two girls you sat between at dinner. Of course the first two, theoretically speaking, offer no problem. Everyone has to dance with them, so you can't be stuck. The girls next to you at dinner are the risk. One or both may be wallflowers. It's best therefore to get the job over with as soon as you get to the dance so the guys on their other sides may be the ones caught."

Len nodded with owl-like gravity. "What about the

mothers of the debutantes honored? Shouldn't I dance with them? Aren't they the real hostesses?"

"It's not compulsory. It's all right if you happen to know them anyway, but otherwise it might look a bit greaseball, a bit too anxious to make a good impression, to be seen whirling two old bags around the dance floor."

"I see. And greaseballs must be very careful not to act like greaseballs."

"I didn't mean it that way, Len."

"No. But I did. What about toasts?"

"Toasts?"

"Well, shouldn't I offer one to my hostess at dinner?"

"No, no. The guy on the deb's right does that, and the one on her left toasts her parents or whoever is giving the party. You won't be seated in either place."

"Why not? Because her best beau would be?"

"No. As a matter of fact, she probably wouldn't put him beside her at all. Too obvious, like fraternity pinning, very middle class. She's apt to have some childhood friend or even a cousin."

"But isn't the idea of a coming out party to introduce one's daughter to the circle of eligible young men from whom she may be expected one day to select a suitable mate?"

"Well, that may have been the case way back. But now the parties have become so vast, with so many friends of friends and so many gate-crashers, that the men may constitute a group from which the parents devoutly pray that she will *not* choose a mate."

"Such as a guy from Newburgh who happens to be visiting one of her guests?"

But I wasn't going to let him have it all his way. "That's it, precisely. We have our guards against the likes of him."

"Watch out! He may get around you. The big mistake was to let him in in the first place."

Len behaved in exemplary fashion that night. He danced with the four girls required, and he remained admirably sober. I was slightly put out that he wanted to stay to the bitter end of the second party, but he at last consented to go home with me at three a.m. He had spoken to all of our classmates who were present, and they had genially introduced him to the most attractive girls on the floor, and by the end of the evening I verily believe that he was acquainted with more of the prominent debutantes of the season than I was.

The same thing went on the next day. At the Piping Rock Club's beach on the Sound, Len induced me to join a rather hungover group of these same classmates and their girls, hashing over the parties of the night before. He ordered a round of martinis, for which he blithely signed my name, and in almost no time we had what seemed to be another party going. This was the first occasion when I noticed that he exercised a peculiar attraction for women. There was something about those mocking eyes in that long pale sober face that seemed at once vaguely to threaten and to titillate them. He varied his conversation with them between amusing compliments, too florid to be taken quite seriously but agreeable to hear, and personal remarks, sometimes daring, even impertinent, but too apt and too funny to be openly resented.

The debutante of the previous night's supper dance, Amanda Gray, was complaining about the newspaper coverage of her party. "How on earth do they manage to dig up all that old family stuff? 'Granddaughter of Mrs. Albert Van Rensselaer Gray and the late Mr. Gray. Great-granddaughter of the late Mrs. X and grandniece of Mrs. Y.' Who cares, in God's name?"

To the astonishment of the group Len uttered a high, piercing scream of a laugh and fell back on the sand as if suddenly convulsed. "Well, if that isn't the most ungrateful thing I ever heard! When your poor mama must have labored an hour on the telephone with some bonehead reporter to get it all straight." Here he sat up and pretended to lift a receiver to his lips to ape remarkably the voice of Mrs. Gray, with whom he couldn't have exchanged more than three words the night before. "Hello, is this the society desk of the *Herald Tribune*? I want to make a correction to the draft I sent you of the notice of my daughter's dance. Yes, and I might just add that I'm a friend of your editor, dear Helen Reid. I'm afraid my secretary described my daughter's paternal grandmother as simply Mrs. Albert V. Gray. No, of course it's not right. It should read Mrs. Albert *Van Rensselaer* Gray. What? Why, certainly it must be changed. And what? You don't want to run that bit about Mr. Gray's being a cotillion leader in the Bachelors Ball of 1899? I'm sorry, I must insist. Do you want me to call Mrs. Reid? No? What? You can't spell Van Rensselaer? And you call yourself a society editor? Really, you people should take courses in American history. All right, I'll spell it for you. V as in Vanderbilt, A as in Astor, N as in nobility —"

Here he was interrupted by a shout of laughter from the whole group. Even poor Amanda had to join in. I wondered for a moment how he could possibly have divined Mrs. Gray's well-known weakness for publicity, and then I recalled, somewhat ruefully, that I had probably told him myself in one of my discourses on the North Shore world that he so astutely encouraged. Of course, with his memory, I might as well have been talking into a recording machine. At any rate, I need not have worried about Amanda. To show what a good sport she could be, she invited me and Len to dine with her at her family's the following night before another supper dance, which was pleasant as we did not have a dinner and it is always hard to sit around at home until midnight.

The rest of the week marked Len's mounting social success, and I really couldn't deny him the pleasure of extending his visit (though my parents had other guests coming) by three more days, as he had received, on his own, three additional invitations. So he moved into my room, and our party season continued, rather longer than I liked. I was now being asked to dances as Len's host by people I didn't know! I didn't mind — at least I believed at the time I didn't — but what I did mind was his behavior at a dinner dance where he and I happened to be seated on either side of a plain, stout female who suffered, as the evening wore on (and wear it did), from a personal defect for which supposed cures were widely advertised in the pharmaceutical market. Long after dinner was over, when I was still dancing with this poor girl, who added speechlessness to her other charms, it began to appear that I should have no respite until she went home with her brother, who might be counted on to perform this task and then return to the party, but who was certainly not going to cut in on her. I sent distress signals to Len, who was whirling around the floor with one beauty after another, but he ignored them all.

When I taxed him severely with this conduct as we drove home from the party in the early morning, his response was quite shameless.

"But I could see that if I'd cut in, I'd have been stuck with her the whole evening. And I've only a few days here. You have all summer."

"But you *knew* I wouldn't have abandoned you. I'd have found someone else to cut in. It might have taken a bit of time, but I'd have done it. Or cut back myself."

"How could I count on that? She was such a horror! To tell the honest truth, I did think once of rescuing you and was actually coming over to do it, but there was such an air of sublime martyrdom plastered all over your mug that I wondered if I might not be risking your salvation in removing its cause."

I decided not to dignify this with a comment. "But even if you were too selfish to rescue me, what about your duty dance? I'll bet you didn't dance with the girl on your other side, either!"

"I most certainly did not. She was almost as bad. You see, I've already discovered that one can't travel very far on your great island without meeting proof that your little rules are flouted right and left. You're like Saint-Simon. You live by an etiquette that nobody follows but yourself."

"Plenty of people follow it!"

"Not the chic types, anyway. I've checked that out. But don't worry. If you write it all down, like the little duke, you'll dominate the history books. His memoirs are the greatest novel ever written. But while you're writing it, I'll be having the better time."

"And that's all that matters, having a better time? There are no rules, no duties, no obligations?"

"Oh, I don't say that. But the better time is paramount."

"I suppose I'm seeing you for the first time," I said bitterly.

"Oh, come now. Haven't you always known? It's not really so much that I need to have a good time myself. On a desert island I might be perfectly content to do nothing at all. It's the idea that someone *else* may be having a better time than I am, and having it shoved in my face, that drives me wild. If it hadn't been for those other guys waltzing around with the prettiest girls and not caring a damn about your duty dances, I'd have come to your aid. Oh, sure, I would. But the way things were, I was damned to hell if I wasn't going to have as good a time as any man in that room!"

Well, what could I say? He had given me a lot to think about.

The following year at Yale, our junior, Len and I roomed together in Davenport. That fall represented the high point of our congeniality. Literature — in our courses, in our theater expeditions to New York, and in our writing for "the Lit" — was now concededly our principal concern, and there were no dances to worry about, at least until Thanksgiving. We made a habit of reading and criticizing each other's stories. Len's were vastly superior to mine. He had a terse, pungent style in his descriptions and a tough wit in his dialogue that took him quite out of the prosy amateurish mire of sentiment from which I was still struggling to escape. The fact that this distinction, so obvious to me, was less so to our fellow editors, offered me further proof that Len was educating me as a critic as well as a writer. And even today, more than four decades later, when I read his stories in my old copies of the magazine, I see that I was right about the promise they showed. My own showed none.

If Len could be devastating in his brief critiques of my work, this only made his rare encomiums the more precious. If he simply said, "That's all right. You've got it now. Don't touch it," my heart would sing. I had never been more sure of anything than that I was rooming with a kind of genius.

Our literary compatability, however, was ultimately soured by just what one might have supposed would have most strengthened it. I began work on a novel and carried it through to completion by spring, working every afternoon in the reading room of the Sterling Library. At first I showed the manuscript to Len as I completed each chapter, but it seemed to elicit so harsh a new note of his critical faculty that I decided at length to keep my work to myself, fearing that his pejorative comments might destroy my creative impulse altogether. Yet my rejection of his "help" seemed only to irritate him further. And then an incident occurred that threatened the very friendship itself.

Len's father went bankrupt, and in a rare display of concern for his only offspring, he transferred to Len five thousand dollars of cash that he had concealed from his creditors. Perhaps he hoped that Len would act as a guardian of the fund, returning it when the coast was clear. If he did he was foiled, for Len, treating the sum as a mere token of what he and his mother were owed, split it between himself and Mrs. Armster. The trouble came when he rather gleefully told me about it. He acted as if he had pulled off a great coup. I tersely pointed out that it was also a fraud on creditors and he might end up in a striped suit.

He was instantly irate. "Don't be ridiculous! The debt he owes me and Mother should have clear priority."

"Has he ever acknowledged it? Do you have a note or letter?"

"Of course not. Are you saying that a man's obligation to support his wife and family has to be in writing?"

"I'm not saying anything. You're the one who's making the assumptions."

"Anyway, there's not the slightest risk. Nobody knows about it. The money was in bills in his apartment."

"What about the girl friend?"

"Oh, she had to be squared, of course. We gave her a G."

"Really, Len! Even if there's no risk, have you no morals?"

"Morals!" He turned almost red, redder anyway than I had ever seen him. He was actually trembling with anger. "It's all very well for you to talk about morals. You've never had to lift a finger to pay for anything, even the Brooks Brothers shirt on your back. You wouldn't find it so easy if you'd had to sweat or smirk for every penny that's ever been spent on you."

"I didn't say it wasn't easy for me. What you're doing doesn't depend on what *I* call it. It's a fraud, and you know it as well as I do."

At this Len gave vent to a blast of resentment that must have been festering within him from the start of what I had deemed our friendship. "I really think you must be the greediest person I've ever known," he said in a tone that was suddenly cold and dry. "You not only want the social world with all its trimmings, you want to go to the chic parties and sneer at the philistines there. And now you're trying to crown your smug superiority with a halo! Really, one has to go back to Dickens to find hypocrites on your scale."

I had no reply to this. I was too hurt. I went to the library to work on my novel, but of course I couldn't write a word. That evening, when we met again, we agreed to have no further discussion of his father's cash. But things were never again quite the same between us. We remained ostensibly close friends, but we tended now, by a sort of tacit agreement, to mingle more with our classmates. If we went to the movies, we would stop to pick up companions in the entry. Len, I suspected, had decided that he had got out of me all that he was going to get. He needed a replacement.

He did, however, in the following spring, give me another example of the highly emotional side of his nature that he usually hid behind the mask of his mockery. I had finished my novel and mailed it off to a famous publishing house, and I had received, after a month of miserable apprehension, a brief but courteous reply rejecting the manuscript though expressing interest in my next effort. The blow had been far greater than I had expected. Perhaps the loneliness of the whole experience — I had told no one of my project after showing the first few chapters to Len — had ill prepared me for the judgment of the world. Now, in a neurotic overreaction, I concluded that I had committed an act of hubris against the gods of my bourgeois forebears and that I must immediately make up for it by turning my back forever on the palace of art, which clearly had no room for me, and joining the ranks of the professional workers. I at once applied for admission to the University of Virginia Law School, the best, I was informed, that would admit me without a college degree, and when accepted, I resigned from Yale. The bewilderment of my poor parents is not relevant to Len's story.

When I broke my news to him, he astonished and dismayed me by bursting into tears. "If you're leaving Yale," he wailed, "it's because of me."

I tried to explain my reasons, but to no avail. He simply shook his head moodily. "I've always had that effect on my friends. I seem to get inside them and destroy them. Perhaps you're smart to get away."

And then, with a sigh and a shrug, as if to dismiss the whole matter as beyond repair, he suddenly suggested a movie. Nor did he ever again revert to the subject of his supposedly malign influence. He was already, I felt sure, inwardly trying to decide with whom he might now most advantageously room in senior year. In fact, he chose well. Bud Dillon was an editor of the *Daily News* (an important post in the Yale of that day) and belonged to an immensely rich Cleveland family. What did Bud see in Len? The opportunity to develop his intellectual side. Oh, yes, we actually made resolutions like that in the 1930s.

Len and I had a less troubled friendship after I left New Haven. We met only on the occasional weekends when I came up from Charlottesville and invited him to stay at my family's apartment in New York. Everything seemed to be going well with him in senior year: he had made many friends among the leaders of the class, his courses amused him, and his grades were brilliant. Indeed, I found his disposition positively sunny. With my retreat into the temple of law all competition between us had ceased. He had no interest in my chosen profession; he was quite willing to abandon to me what he considered a "picky trade." His conversation was wholly about the world that I had left; my new life was a blank to him. But that was characteristic of Len. I don't think that he believed that I, or any of his friends, really existed when we were away from him.

I always remembered what he had said about my greediness, and I wondered if what had made him so angry with me had been the idea that I was going to have more fun than he. It may have seemed to him that, equipped with financial and social security and launched upon what he chose to predict as my successful career at the bar, I had quite enough, and that it was only fair that I should leave the joys and pangs of creative writing to the Leonard Armsters of this world. Even my poor novel must have somehow threatened him. Had I succeeded in publishing it, I would have added to the delights of my "social position" the heady joy of seeing my words in print between hard covers. It might have been almost too much for him.

•　•　•

Len, however, after his graduation from Yale, did not embark directly on a career of creative writing. The family of his new roommate owned a controlling interest in the weekly newsmagazine *Globe*, and he was offered a job there as a reporter. So well did he do that he was signing his own articles after only four months. Bud Dillon had taken a job with Guaranty Trust Company, and he rented a bedroom in his new Manhattan penthouse to Len, who became a cohost at all the parties given there. From my viewpoint in Charlottesville it looked as if Len had already achieved both the social and career successes that he had coveted.

It was at a dance on the long Thanksgiving weekend in New York that I had the satisfaction of being able to tell Len the name of the most beautiful girl in the room. He still did not know quite everything.

"Oh, that's Clover Kip. I'm surprised you didn't know. Actually, she's my second cousin. Would you like to meet her?"

"Very much indeed."

One of the reasons that I had immediately mentioned my relationship was that Clover rather insisted on it. She had told me candidly that she had no need of more beaux, but, as an only child and one who tended to be impatient with her own sex (particularly at the debutante age), she had a very definite need of friends. Our kinship, she claimed, though distant by New York standards, was the perfect basis for a conversational intimacy that might prove mutually valuable without leading to romance. I never regretted accepting the proposed connection, for

Clover was simply the best company in the world. Although no heiress and unable to give a large party, she had been, two years before, the most popular debutante of the season. She had everything: charm, blond beauty, brains, a radiant cheerfulness, and even a serious liberal bent, on which she much insisted — a New Dealer in anti–New Deal New York. But she was never a bore about it. She was perfectly willing to enjoy, nay, even to revel in the beautiful dresses and all the good times that seemed so necessary a part of the "coming out" process and its aftermath. "I relish the old while working for the new," she would retort to persons small enough to tax her with this.

Len, I thought, made a fool of himself that night. He went through the almost clownish contortions of being violently smitten, and he cut in on Clover six or seven times on the dance floor, even cutting back in on men who had cut in on him, a thing that was not done, form requiring that one should wait until the girl had had at least two intervening partners. I apologized to Clover for his lack of manners when I danced with her, but she did not seem to mind.

"He certainly has a funny tone," she admitted. "But I think I like him. Is he as bright as he seems?"

"What makes him seem so?"

"He makes such a wicked satire of my supposed popularity. He says I've given myself to the mob when I should be reserved for the cognoscenti. In short, that I've cast my pearls before swine."

"Len can be an awful ass at times."

"But, you know, I think he's right. I *have* cared about being popular. I'm like a millionaire who's always looking for more millions."

"Isn't that the nature of the beast?"

"But it doesn't have to be! Your friend says I place myself at the mercy of every little man who has two dirty hands to clap."

"I suppose he wants you all to himself."

"He can want what he wants. That's hardly a concern of mine."

I had to return to Charlottesville immediately thereafter, but Len, who for all his eccentricities was a faithful correspondent, kept me abreast of the progress of his new friendship. I naturally felt some jealousy that he should be taking over so quickly my own role of confidant, but there was a rather nasty solace in the candor with which Clover herself wrote of him:

> Your pal, Leonard, has become a curiously intimate part of my life. He calls me every day, sometimes just to chat. As he has his eyes and ears open to the world and picks up every item of news from the state of the Cold War to the latest adultery in Gotham, I admit to being intrigued. And then he has courtesy seats for every show and passes to every gallery opening. Or sometimes he just escorts me to one of the courses I'm taking at Columbia. As a roving reporter he seems able to make time to do anything he wants. He's like a genie: I rub a lamp and there he is, grinning and asking, 'What is your wish, Princess?' It doesn't even bother me that he claims to be passionately in love. In the first place, I don't for a

moment believe it. It's rather a kind of act or panto-
mime that for some reason he feels obliged to put on.
And, secondly, he never embarrasses me in public or
tries to maul me in private. If he did, I should certainly
send him packing, as I cannot imagine returning his
sentiment, sham or real. I hope I'm not such a cave girl
as to require nothing but muscle and brawn in a man,
but I need a bit more of those things than our friend
possesses.

It was hard to be jealous of poor Len after reading this.
Imagine how he would have felt had he been looking over
my shoulder! Anyway, not long after I received this letter, he did something that destroyed forever any remote
chance he may have had to make headway in my cousin's
affections. He introduced her to Munroe Leake, a thirty-
five-year-old junior partner in the Cravath firm with
whom he had become friendly while writing an article
for *Globe* on Wall Street corporation lawyers.

Munroe, unfortunately for Len, proved to be just the
man Clover was waiting for. He looked like a successful
attorney in a movie, handsome, dark complexioned, square
jawed, who seemed able to handle anything from an
argument before the U.S. Supreme Court to the fixing of
a traffic ticket. And he was as cultivated as he was effi-
cient; he had read all the new books and performed
creditably on the piano. Oh, and I almost forgot, he
played polo at Meadowbrook. Really, it was almost too
much.

And yet Len seemed to take a certain pride, when next
we met, in what he had done, as if he had been under

some aesthetic obligation to bring two such beautiful human beings together, if only to show them to the world as partners on the dance floor. When a strong attachment almost immediately began to make itself evident between the two, he purported to be distressed at his foolhardiness, but I wasn't a bit sure that the satisfaction of having been the originator of so spectacular a romance in society did not compensate him for any disappointment in love. I was less sure myself that Munroe was such a good thing for Clover. I wondered if there might not be a touch of brutality in his need to take over so lovely a creature as she. I even found it in me to speculate that Len might be titillated by this. Certainly, as the romance flourished, and people began to look for the announcement of an engagement, Len was constantly seen in the company of the interesting couple. The trio was even dubbed a kind of platonic "design for living," after the Noel Coward comedy about a less innocent threesome.

In the next months Len began to drink much more than usual. According to Clover, my faithful correspondent, he imbibed only at parties, but he went to a great many of these. When intoxicated, he would wax highly excited and emotional, and this state would soon be followed by one of deep depression.

Munroe is beginning to get sick and tired of him," Clover complained. "I hate to leave poor Len out of things, but I have to consider Munroe, for (confiden-

tially) he is now my fiancé. And when he makes up his
mind about something, he can be very firm indeed.
Can't you use your influence on Len and get him to
behave himself?

I tried, but with little result. Len wrote rather huffily
that Munroe was being stuffy over a trifle, and that most
people found him more amusing after "a couple of
drinks." As my school work was very taxing at this time,
I endeavored to put the problem out of my mind. I
thought I could count on Munroe at length to separate
Clover and Len altogether, and that this would bring Len
to his senses.

But it was not long before another letter from Clover
brought news of further deterioration in the situation.

Munroe and I are formally announcing our engagement a week from Tuesday, at a cocktail party given by
Mummy and Daddy, and I want you to come up for it.
I know that's an awful lot to ask, but I'll be in your
debt for a big favor whenever you choose to call it. The
truth is that Len is behaving so peculiarly that I'm
afraid he'll do something awful at the party, and I need
you there to keep an eye on him. Munroe made a row
about my asking him, but for once I insisted on having
my way. Len at times strikes me as almost irrational. He
even talks wildly about following us on the honeymoon.
Of course it's just a lot of nonsense, and anyway, *Globe*
is sending him abroad next month as a war correspondent, so that should take care of the problem. Just see us
through the party, dearest coz; that's all I shall need.

I was thoroughly disgusted, as exams were upon me, but I could hardly refuse such an appeal. It also irritated me that Len, who was causing all this fuss, should apparently be rewarded with a glamorous assignment in Europe. I reflected bitterly that everything and everybody seemed obliged to contribute to his eternal "good times." Would Armageddon provide him with his ultimate delight?

I arranged on the telephone with Len that I should fly up to New York on the day of the party and go to it with him. I went straight from the airport to Bud Dillon's penthouse, where I found Len alone in the bar. Unfortunately, he had already had several drinks, and I was quite unable to keep him from having another. His mood was somber but detached; he treated me almost as a stranger, yet a stranger to whom, because of his very indifference, he could relate even intimate things.

"This marriage may seem to some the finest work of art I shall ever have achieved," he observed. "Or to others as my first, perhaps my only, failure. In either case, it may mark a fit ending to my life in this great nation."

I assumed he was referring to his approaching departure for England. "I don't see why you take it for granted that you were the sole cupid in the affair. They might perfectly well have met without you."

He shook his head gloomily. "Never. They had to meet through me. They had to show me something."

"Are you really so smitten with Clover? She thought you were putting it on a bit."

His stare was long and cold. But when he answered me, his tone was almost matter-of-fact. "She was wrong. I'm in love with both of them."

"Oh really, Len, must everything be a melodrama?"

Again he shook his head. "It is unfortunately no melodrama," he said, as if musing to himself. "It's like being in love with love, or being in love with the most beautiful thing this benighted world can offer. And what is that but the mutual delight, the mutual ecstasy of two such creatures when they mate? I want to make love to Clover and I want to make love to Munroe; there are different parts of me that thrust me in each direction, but it sometimes seems to me that what I really want is to make love to both of them simultaneously — oh, I don't mean a balling or anything like that — it's more that I want to be somehow invisibly between them. I want to *be* their love, for isn't that the greatest pleasure in the world?"

"And one you're still missing?" My exasperation at his incessant greed for amusement made me cruel. "But isn't it always true that when a man has bisexual feelings, the one for his own sex is the real one?"

He actually smiled. "Meaning that I'm nothing but a fantasizing fairy? Oh, I've taught you well. You really know how to dish it out!"

Shamed by my own malevolence, I had nothing to say. All I could do was suggest that we go on to the party at once. But Len simply shook his head and went to the little bar to pour himself another drink. His back as he did so was to be my last sight of him.

He never came to Clover's party, and when I went to bed that night I thought it was just as well he hadn't. But early the next morning, my smugness and complacency were finally shattered by Clover's tense voice on the telephone. Len was dead. He had gone to another party, in Greenwich Village, where he had sat, very drunk, on a window seat by an open window, talking and laughing rather wildly, with a girl he had just met. Tilting back and forth as he told her a funny story, he had suddenly seemed to lose his balance and had fallen backward into the street four stories below.

Len, born a Catholic, received the full rites of the church, as there was no evidence that his death was other than accidental. But I received this letter in the next day's post, which he must have written after I had left Bud Dillon's apartment and mailed on his way to the Village party:

> When you read this, you may regret your last words to me. Don't. Your rather childish but understandable pique had nothing to do with a decision already taken. I purchased the revolver a week ago. Read over that poem of Housman's that we once discussed at Yale: "Shot so quick, so clean an ending." Not encumbered as I have been, you should have a good life. Don't regret our quarrels. They meant very little to either of us. Cheers!

There were several things wrong with this letter. In the first place, his fall from the window had the appearance of an accident or spontaneous act; no gun or other indication of premeditation was found among his effects. Second, I could not recall ever discussing any work of A. E. Housman with him. The verses in question offer the poet's grim congratulations to a young suicide who has evidently dreaded that his hitherto repressed homosexual inclinations, once yielded to, would disgrace him and corrupt the objects of his affection. The first stanza reads:

> Shot so quick, so clean an ending,
> Oh, that was right, lad, that was brave.
> Yours was not an ill for mending;
> 'Twas best to take it to the grave.

I could not believe that Len would have been much concerned with his own sexual morals or those of any partner in an affair. He had always struck me as totally free of any guilt feelings in such matters. The subsequent lines, "You would not live to wrong your brothers" and "Souls undone, undoing others," would seem to have nothing to do with the moral climate in which he breathed. Indeed, had he lived to learn the recently discovered facts of Housman's clandestine trips across the Channel to meet male prostitutes, he would have been the first to laugh gleefully at the rank hypocrisy of the poet. But there is one stanza that may have come closer to his own case:

> Oh, you had forethought, you had reason,
> And saw your road and where it led,
> And early wise and brave in season
> Put the pistol to your head.

Len may have foreseen the ultimate solution of his sexual problem and hated it, not for any moral grounds, but because the acts resulting, the physical unions, may have struck him as ugly, fatally lacking in the grace and exquisiteness that he chose to see in the coming together of two such beings as Clover and Munroe. I recalled how deeply he had always admired the verse of the Jesuit poet Gerard Manley Hopkins, who had been guilty of the heresy, at least in my opinion, of identifying God with physical beauty, not only in a landscape but in the male human body. Len may have differed from him only in substituting art for God. When one put together two facts: that he saw pleasure as the principal goal in life and that he saw beauty as pleasure, one might deduce his inevitable decision not to live in a world where he was denied the greatest pleasure he could visualize.

Orlando Hatch

I MET HIM in my first term at Virginia Law School, and I liked him immediately. I have never known anyone to exude the same degree of warm, confident friendliness. He came from Petersburg, but he was by no means an "FFV" (First Families of Virginia). His father ran a small jewelry store and had had to make considerable sacrifices to put his oldest son through law school. Indeed Orlando's six younger siblings had had to do without a professional education. Unlike my lineaged Richmond friends, he was ignorant of many of the traditions of the Old South and even of some of the major battles of the Civil War; I heard him once refer to "the day those damn Yankees fired on Fort Sumter." But at the same time he was amiably convinced of the absolute rectitude of all Virginian causes and pleasantly unimpressed by any "big doings" further north.

He seemed indeed to have no animosities, except where his very pretty girl friend, Elisa, was concerned. When she came up from Petersburg to go to a dance with him at his fraternity, I observed that he never took his eyes off her and would, in a courteous but firm manner, warn off any man who cut in on her more than once. It was obvious that he would not hesitate, should he deem it necessary, to use his fists. Yet I suspected even then that Elisa's character had none of his own strong base.

He was remarkably handsome, with a tight muscular build and the walk of a cat. His hair was a jumble of small blond curls; his eyes sky blue; his jaw, under a fixed half smile, assertive rather than aggressive. He might have been ignorant of the battles of the past, but he put me in mind of a daguerreotype of a young Confederate soldier — one who might not return from the front. Yet there was certainly no corresponding sadness in his own later career as a Navy pilot in the Second World War, which he survived, as he seemed to survive everything, without a scratch.

For that was the thing about Orlando. He could cope with any situation. He seemed to take it serenely for granted that a mellow humor and pleasant manners and the treatment of other people as men of good will like himself would open the doors of any class or caste. Open them? Were they not already gaping? And indeed I was to see the FFVs take him in, the leaders of Wall Street take him in, even the "jet set" of Long Island's North Shore seek (without great success) to clasp him to their bosoms.

"Do you know something, Dan?" he asked me, a few years ago, as we were lunching in his big office before the panorama of New York harbor. "I find that kind of dirty dealing almost impossible to understand." We were discussing the latest embezzlement scandal. "Maybe it's because I've never been tempted to commit a crime. I don't say I'm naturally virtuous. I may even be naturally crooked. But how can I tell till old Satan tries me? He seems to have left me off his list."

"He knows he'd be wasting his time."

"Not at all. It's simply that it's always struck me that the straight way of doing things is apt to be the paying way."

It was amusing to speculate that Orlando might have turned his back on the devil, shut him deliberately out of his sight. Could he have been *afraid* of temptation? I recalled a discussion we had had at law school about my northern aversion to the strict requirements of the honor code. Would he really have turned in his best friend, I asked him, as we were pledged to do, had he caught him cheating on an examination?

"Well, I make it a point not to look around the room during a test," he replied. "That way I avoid any embarrassing situations."

Had it been the same during the war in Vietnam, when he had served briefly as an assistant secretary of defense? He had initially professed to see in our intervention the attempt to rescue a free people from an imposed communist tyranny, and even after his resignation, which was widely rumored to have been motivated by his disillusionment with the American cause, he had refused to denounce the war. All he would say was that a former officer of the government should keep his mouth shut.

But it still seemed to me that he was right about his life having been largely immune to temptation, at least to the kind of temptation dangled before those who have to do with the stock market. As a young clerk and junior partner in the Wall Street law firm of Arnold & Degener, where we had both been associates, and later as a partner and president of Russell Brothers, the investment bankers, he had labored almost exclusively in the offering or underwriting of giant issues of securities, an area carefully monitored by Uncle Sam's commissioners, for clients who were paid too well for being straight to contemplate being crooked. He had not even had to have private means to become a partner of Russell Brothers, for that wealthy firm had allowed him an ample period in which to contribute his required portion of capital. It was perfectly possible in the Wall Street of his day for a man to climb what Disraeli called the "greasy pole" of success without getting his hands dirty.

Orlando and I graduated from law school in 1941, and we both went directly into the Navy. We had both also accepted jobs in Arnold & Degener, which would have to wait for peace. I saw Orlando only twice during the war, running into him quite by chance at officers' clubs in Ulithi and Leyte. He was always the same, delighted to see me, casual about his missions and showing none of the condescension of the "real" Navy for those ponderous marine trucks, the LSTs, on which I served. Despite the presence on both occasions of fellow pilots and even of friendly superior officers, he showed no disposition to sit and drink with anyone but me. It was one of his charms never to betray — or perhaps not even to feel — the need to improve the company in which he found himself. Only on the last time that I saw him, shortly before V-J Day, did he differ from his usual self; he seemed actually depressed.

"But you're going home on leave!" I exclaimed in astonishment when he confessed to his mood. "What more could a man ask?"

"It's Elisa, Dan. She's only written me once in the past three months."

"Maybe her letters didn't get through."

He shook his head. "I'm not kidding myself. She's found someone else."

I stared. "How could she do better than what she's got? A devoted swain with the Silver Star? The hero of the home town? Good Lord, man, if she liked you before, she must like you even more now."

"Things don't always work out that way. Some gals just can't wait. It's the old case of a bird in hand."

"I won't hear you say that about my friend Elisa!"

He smiled ruefully. "I appreciate your spirit. But I'm afraid I can't share your optimism. My ma's letters have contained some pretty dark hints about Elisa and a Marine bastard home on sick leave. Wounded in Okinawa."

"Fatally, I hope."

"No such luck. Just a scratch. Just enough for a Purple Heart."

"Well, he'd better watch out, when you get home. He'll wish he was back out here."

"No, I'm not like that any more, Dan. I know I used to be kind of rough with some of the jerks who were trying to fool around with her. But that was when I thought she cared for me. Once that's gone, it's gone for good. If she wants this guy, she's welcome to him."

"But, Orly, after all these years! Surely this is just a passing fancy on her part."

"Well, if that's all it is, okay. But I'm afraid it's a lot more than that. And I've had warnings before — even before the war, if the truth be told. Elisa has always complained that I want to own her."

As I looked at him now, his cap tilted back on his head, his eye fixed bemusedly on his whiskey glass, lean and bronzed by the Pacific sun, I marveled that any girl who had once liked him should not like him now. But then I reminded myself that Elisa wasn't seeing him now.

"Well, if it should be true, when you come to New York after all this is over, I'll see to it that you meet plenty of gals just as attractive as Elisa."

"Oh, when all this is over," he muttered in a sudden fit of disgust. "Maybe it'll never be over. And maybe that'll be just as well. For some of us, anyway."

But the very next week the first of the two big bombs was dropped, and it was only a matter of months before Orlando and I were sharing an office at Arnold & Degener, for all the world as if the mighty conflict had never occurred. His prediction about Elisa had been correct. By the time he got back to Petersburg she had already married her Marine — probably, I have always suspected, to have a defense against the renewal of his suit. She would not be "owned" by Orlando or any other man. There are some women who would rather be unhappy than secure, and it has always a bit gratified an unpleasant side of my nature that Elisa *has* been thoroughly unhappy. She is now, I've been told, obese, and drinks. I shouldn't be surprised if Orlando supports her, but that, of course, he would never tell me.

Law clerks were paid very little in 1946, and Orlando lived with two other Virginia men in a small flat off Washington Square. He never complained about his treatment by Elisa, nor were their any signs of self-pity or depression, but he showed little interest in social life and seemed perfectly content to work most of his nights and weekends, opportunities for which our employers were only too ready to provide.

I had told him that I would introduce him to girls, and I did, to several of the most attractive I knew, but although he was always pleasant and even courtly, in his grave, Southern way, and although they invariably found him charming, no intimacy developed. I had almost decided I had better give up and wait till his "mourning" period was over when Zoe Cobb, who had heard about him from another girl, asked me if I couldn't arrange a meeting.

"He sounds so mysterious!" she exclaimed, clapping her hands when I agreed to do so. "And I hear he does nothing but work. Perhaps I can lure him from it."

I looked at her doubtfully. I couldn't remember her ever asking me to introduce her to a man before. She had always seemed somehow self-sufficient. "But suppose you fall in love with him?"

"What if I do?"

"And he remains pining for his old love?"

"Oh, come off it, Dan. Isn't that just the challenge every girl is waiting for?"

Zoe and I had been friends from childhood, and there had been a time when I had fancied myself in love with her. But she had neither returned my affection nor professed really to believe in it; she had insisted that nothing like that was in the cards for us, and couldn't we, please, just stay good friends? Which, surprisingly enough, in view of the blow to my vanity, we had. But then Zoe was simply the nicest girl in the world, not beautiful certainly, but with a friendly, frank, freckled face, a sharply perceiving mind, and a generous heart. She had never, so far as I knew, been seriously in love with anyone, and she was now twenty-five. Yet she was as rich as she was good-natured, and several men had wanted to marry her, but there had always been something almost fiercely independent about her. I had classified her as one of those souls who are ready to put themselves out for others but never to give themselves.

And now she proceeded to fall head over heels in love

with Orlando at their very first meeting. It was as if she had been waiting all along for the fairy prince and recognized him as soon as he appeared. And Orlando? What did he feel? He seemed charmed by her, but then he was too innately Virginian not to seem charmed by every girl he met. What, however, was different in this new relationship was that he found a way to alter his schedule of work so as to be able to take Zoe out at least twice a week. Was it love? Would he begin to show himself truculently possessive, as he had with Elisa? But he didn't. Perhaps he had simply matured. Or perhaps he had learned his lesson.

"Things seem to be going pretty fast between you and Zoe," I observed one day at lunch.

"She is sure one lovely girl."

"I quite agree. She's always laughing, but she can be very serious, too."

"Isn't that good?"

"Of course . . ."

"But what?"

"But she can be seriously hurt."

"Dan!" His eyes mocked me. "You know I'd never hurt a fly."

And that was all I could get out of him. In the office, however, one of our fellow associates was odious about what he termed Orlando's "rebel luck."

"Those mush-mouthed Southerners always end up with their paws in a pot of gold."

"And what do you mean by *that*?"

"They marry dough. More power to them. I only wish I had."

Well, I confess something like the same idea had pushed its crude way past the barriers of my own mind. Zoe was certainly a very good match for a young man from Petersburg without a dime over his small salary and coming from a family that could hardly be expected to appeal to Zoe's snobbish mother. And yet, I reminded myself, he had been passionately anxious to marry Elisa, who had offered him even less social advantages than he already possessed. True. But still, hadn't I always, deep down, suspected a tough core under that quiet charm?

If the same nasty suspicion had entered the head of Mrs. Cobb, she did not seem in the least put off by it. To my astonishment she thoroughly approved of her daughter's admirer. She was the very opposite of Zoe, tall, cool, with a long handsome oval face, seemingly made of marble, exquisitely dressed and socially confined to a tight little group of old New York rich. But on a weekend at the Piping Rock Club, passing me in the corridor, she suddenly stopped.

"Danny. Have you a few minutes? How about a game of backgammon?"

It was obviously a pretext. After she rolled her dice, having won the first throw, she looked up at me quizzically.

"I like your friend Hatch."

"He's a great guy."

"And I'm very grateful to you for introducing him to Zoe. If something comes of it, I don't mind saying I'll owe you one."

"Really?"

"That surprises you?"

"A bit."

"Why, may I ask?"

"Well, he doesn't strike me as having exactly the background a loving New York mother would want."

"A loving New York mother or Zoe Cobb's mother?"

"Both, I guess."

"I've heard all about the jewelry store in Petersburg. He makes no secret of it, which is all to his credit. And I assume the parents are impossible. Never mind. Hatch is the kind of young man who will leave them behind without in the least rejecting them or even hurting their feelings. For there's not a vulgar bone in his body. He has the instinct of how to do things."

"Ah, you see that."

"Don't *you* see it?"

"Of course."

"Well, do you think I'm so much dumber than you, Danny Ruggles?"

"Oh no. But you haven't had my chances to observe him."

"Maybe I'm smarter. Women often are in these matters. It's perfectly all right to be ambitious for your children if you're not stupid about it, as unfortunately most parents are. If you want a successful son-in-law you should be able to pick him out. Orlando Hatch will be just that."

I agreed, but I was still surprised by her perspicacity.

"And he'll be a good husband," I asserted stoutly. She looked at me shrewdly, as if to make out what I might be implying.

"And if he's not, no one will ever know. Least of all Zoe."

Things worked out pretty much as Mrs. Cobb had predicted, certainly so far as Zoe's happiness and Orlando's success were concerned. Zoe adored her husband, and he seemed more than adequately devoted, even when, as the years passed, he almost unnaturally retained his good looks (the gray curls that ultimately replaced the blond ones were just as becoming) while she became a little too round-faced and just a wee bit too stout. Intimate though I was in their home, I never heard them quarrel. When Orlando spoke of Zoe wanting this or that, it always seemed to be taken for granted that she should get it, and she spoke the same way of him.

I resigned from Arnold & Degener in the same year that Orlando was made a junior partner, not out of jealousy or disappointment, but to try my hand at being a full-time writer. When I discovered that greater concentration did not improve the quality of my fiction, I returned to the firm, but that was three years later. In the meantime Orlando had also left it, but with his bosses' blessing, to become a partner of Russell Brothers, their principal client. By the time he was forty-five he had accumulated a fortune many times larger than his wife's, and the passage of another decade found him one of the most considerable financial figures of the city.

He and Zoe lived handsomely but never ostentatiously. They bought a small pretty red-brick Queen Anne manor house in Locust Valley on the North Shore of Long Island and a commodious apartment on Park Avenue, furnished in conventional eighteenth-century English style. Everything they had was good and immaculately maintained; nothing was unusual or even very interesting, for neither of them had much concern with the decor of life. They wanted to be comfortable and to be able to entertain easily; they had no desire to have possessions that would intrude on their lives. Zoe had always been too down-to-earth to care much for the frills of social life, but she found the milieu in which they moved — that of public-spirited, largely self-made members of the old financial houses who were constantly interrupting their money-making to take high federal jobs or to raise funds for museums or universities — agreeable to her taste and conscience. And indeed I myself found it pleasant, at their parties, to feel that the luxury of the background was tempered with a sense of good works and serious thinking. A Russell Brothers partner who did nothing but pile up cash for himself was eyed a bit askance.

The way Orlando and Zoe treated his mother was another example of the attractive way in which they did things. When old Mrs. Hatch, now a widow and hand-somely supported in Petersburg by her son, came to visit them in Locust Valley, she was made much of by both and somehow presented as a noble character who had raised a large family against untold adversities. I don't know quite how it was done, for no actual misstatements were ever made, but guests, I believe, went away with the impression that Mrs. Hatch, gun in hand, had fought off marauders in an Appalachian wilderness rather than en-joyed the quiet life of suburban Petersburg. The jeweler's wife had become a kind of Elizabeth Zane.

I have said that Orlando and Zoe never quarreled, but they did have differences of opinion, which they would patiently thrash out to a usually harmonious resolution. These differences were largely over their son, Tommy, on the subject of whom Zoe struck me as decidedly more de-tached than her husband.

Not everybody liked Tommy. I did not, though I took great and (I believe) successful pains to conceal the fact, but my wife did. She felt the young man bore a heavy load in being Orly's son. Alice Kay and I had married ten years after the Hatches, and as she was a dozen years younger than I, Zoe must have initially struck her as a matron of an almost different generation. The difference in age was compounded by that of occupation: Alice was a busy professional fund raiser for major hospitals, and Zoe, oddly enough, in view of her husband's many activi-ties, did nothing but sit on a couple of sleepy "old New York" charity boards. As this seemed perfectly to satisfy both her and Orly, however, only a fanatical feminist would have objected. Alice was not quite that. She and Zoe formed the pleasant, temperate friendship of sensible wives faced with an old and indissoluble bond between their husbands.

"What do you and Orly talk about at your weekly lunches?" Alice asked me once.

"Oh, everything. Law, politics, the stock market. My writing. His golf game."

"But not personal things?"

"That's never been Orly's way."

"Because he has something to hide?"

"Now what makes you say a thing like that?"

"The fact that he's too perfect."

"And that's a fault?"

"I should say it was a whopper."

"You don't really like Orly, do you?"

"Oh, but I do. Probably rather more than you want me to. Orly has no difficulty being liked by women. It's just that I see things in him — or about him — that you may have known him too long to notice."

"Such as?"

"Well, for one, he's possessive. I suppose he can't help it. He absorbs people, like a sponge."

"Would you say he's absorbed me?"

Alice reflected. "No. It's not your function to be absorbed. Even assuming you could be. Your function is to reassure him."

"Of what?"

She smiled. "Perhaps, precisely, that he's not posses-sive!"

"So you think he suspects it?"

"How could he not, being as smart as he is? And sus-pecting it, mustn't he fear that some day the possessed will rise in rebellion?"

"You mean Zoe?"

"Heavens no. She loves to be possessed. She's secure. I mean, of course, Tommy. It's a pity they had only one child, and that a son. A mean kittenish little daughter might have been able to handle Orly."

Tommy had his father's blond, muscular good looks, though one was aware of a possible future fleshiness from which Orlando had been exempted. And he had a portion of his father's charm, though it was blurred, or perhaps I should say a trifle vulgarized, by a heartiness, an over-emphatic friendliness, a too pronounced eye contact as he would make some remark such as (to me): "I know you are one of Dad's closest friends, and I hope I may come to you with any problem as I would to him. I shall always be the better for your wisdom, Dan." Tommy — immaculate in dark tweeds with a scarlet tie, striding into the lobby of Russell Brothers, or brilliant as a peacock in a gaudy blazer at the Piping Rock beach, or at the Belmont races complete with derby, cigar, and binoculars — Tommy was almost too much the society fashion plate, the sleek stal-lion richly caparisoned, with a whiff of caricature of the Edwardian dandy. And his braying, almost Celtic roar of a laugh struck me as having been intended to reveal the essential beast beneath the trappings of that glittering armor and to reassure the female of the species, including his kittenish little wife (very much like Alice's concept of a daughter for Orly).

Tommy's marks had been far from brilliant at Harvard, but he had always managed to squeak through each step of the expensive private educational process. Since it has always been an acceptable practice in investment banking to bring in a son to share the family capital, nobody had been surprised when Orlando had taken him into Russell Brothers. Tommy's hours were never extended into nights or weekends, but he made his presence colorfully known at the better country clubs, at the races, and on Southern shooting plantations. It was generally assumed that he made up for any deficiency as a market analyst by bringing in business, and that Orlando Hatch, as usual, knew just what he was doing.

Zoe never openly downgraded her son or implied that his father had pushed him too much, but when people praised him to her face — which they were apt to do, on the natural assumption that any mother would be proud of so popular a child — she would confine her reaction to a rather stiff nod.

If Tommy was "possessed" by his father, his wife was distinctly less so. Edith Hatch was inclined to be resentful of her father-in-law, whom she accused of acting as "chairman of the board" of her life. One Saturday night, when Alice and I were weekending in Locust Valley and the young Hatches, who lived down the road in a house

Orlando had given them, came to dinner, Edith's resent-ment erupted in a rather ugly scene.

"I have a bone to pick with you, Mr. Hatch," she said shortly after we were seated at the table. "I have been told, by what I consider a reliable source, that it was at *your* request that Tommy was not given the Paris job by his firm."

"Don't you think, Edie," Orlando replied mildly, "that my partners are capable of making up their own minds as to whom they send to Paris, without consulting me?"

"I didn't say they weren't. But we all know they're going to honor your wish. *Did* you let them know you wanted Tommy here?"

"I said he was more valuable to Russell Brothers here, yes."

"Oh, Mr. Hatch, you're really too awful! You *know* I was pining for a year in Paris. Can't you ever let us run our own lives? Must you always be tightening the leash around our necks? Tommy and I might as well be a couple of poodles."

Zoe at once sprang to Orlando's defense. "I haven't noticed that you're so independent of your father-in-law when it comes to accepting his bounty," she retorted. "It seems to me that poodle's paw is pretty constantly out-stretched."

"Oh, Mrs. Hatch, you always take his side. You won't understand there's a string to every gift he makes. If he pays our club dues it's got to be *his* club. If he gives us a house it's got to be next door. A string, did I say? It's a goddam ball and chain!"

"Edith, I really won't sit by and hear you take that tone to your father-in-law. Must we expose the Ruggleses to a family ruckus? Let us talk of something else. The weather. Anything."

I noted that Tommy had not offered a word.

Our dinner passed with considerable constraint, and the young Hatches departed almost immediately afterward. But in our room, after an evening of bridge, Alice expressed some sympathy for Edith.

"I admit that she made herself singularly unpleasant. But of course Tommy had put her up to it. How else can he handle a father who's always in the right? A parent should show some weaknesses, so the poor offspring can develop their fangs."

The following morning, while Orlando and I were waiting for the foursome ahead of us on the Piping Rock golf course to tee off, he returned to the subject of the previous night's discussion.

"There's something I'd like to explain to you, Dan. I couldn't say it before Alice and Zoe, because I don't want them to know. But I don't care to have you think I'm a possessive dad who would keep his daughter-in-law from the Paris of her dreams because he finds it handy to have her husband at his beck and call."

"I *don't* think so."

"I've got to have Tommy where I can keep an eye on him. He's not good enough for the league he's playing in — the league Edith *wants* him to play in. The league she'd be sore as hell if he wasn't playing in. And imagine what the poor guy's life would be like with Edith sore! So I've had to see not only that he's a partner in the firm, but that he's backed up by people good enough to check him out. And *that* has taken some doing."

"I should think so!"

"Everybody's pride has to be saved. Not only Tommy's and Edith's, but that of all my partners. I've had to learn to be subtle, Dan. And now you see why I couldn't let Tommy out of my sight to make a jackass of himself in Paris."

The group ahead of us was now moving on. I hung back for just a minute. "There's still one thing I don't see. Why don't you tell Zoe?"

"Do you think she doesn't *know?*"

So that was it. That was their bone of contention. Zoe didn't believe that Tommy need be so protected from the world. Alice was right. Tommy should have been given the chance to sharpen his own fangs and claws.

But *was* it that which brought about the final catastrophe? Does nature really have any need of sharpening the weapons of its predators? May they not even be like razors if kept untouched?

I was sitting in my office in Arnold & Degener when my secretary told me that Mr. Hatch was in the reception hall.

"Why doesn't he come in?" I asked, thinking it was Orlando, who as a regular client and former partner had the run of the office. "Send him up."

I looked up to see Tommy closing my door behind him. He took a seat, very deliberately, before my desk.

"I have come to you, Dan, as Dad's oldest friend. There is some pretty bad news I want you to tell him."

Tommy evidently enjoyed dramatic pauses, for he eyed me now beadily during one so protracted that I finally struck the top of my desk impatiently. "Please, Tommy, out with it. Is it a death in the family?"

His expression seemed distorted between a grimace and a smirk. "Worse than that, I'm afraid."

"What?"

"I'm about to be indicted. Embezzlement. From three clients' accounts. Two of them my old man's. Of course he'll make them good. But that won't help me."

I was about to ask him why he hadn't gone to Orly, but then I knew. I closed my eyes, as if to ease the gashing pain of it. "Oh, my God! There has to be some mistake."

"There's no mistake. I was hocked up to my neck. If I'd gotten away to Paris, I'd never have come back. But that wasn't to be, I guess."

"Tommy, *why?*"

He looked away glumly. "I don't know. I've never known. Will you go and tell him? Now? Before it hits the evening headlines?"

What more could I say? I grabbed my hat and left him sitting in my office.

But on my rapid way down Wall Street to Russell Brothers I saw the headlines of an "Extra." I was too late. The receptionist, with a long face, told me that Mr. Hatch would see no one.

"Except Mr. Ruggles," came a voice from behind her. It was Orlando's secretary, who had been waiting for me. She took me to his office where I found him smoking a pipe, perfectly impassive.

"I knew you were on the way over. I telephoned your office."

"Oh, Orly, it's so horrible! But you don't seem surprised."

"Because I've always known."

I stared. "You mean he's done it before?"

"Well, not this particular thing, no. At least I don't think so. Sit down, Dan. It'll help me to talk about it. To the only person I can. Except Zoe, of course. She knows all about it, too. And all the things that have led up to it. From way, way back." I sat down, without a word, facing away from him, as if I were the patient and he the analyst. As always with Orlando, he seemed the one in greater control. "When he was a little kid, no more than eight or nine, he used to steal. It went on a long time before I caught it. First toys of his pals, then stamps from fellow collectors, soon bright little objects from stores. Unfortunately, or fortunately, one of my partners, after a weekend, mentioned to me that he was missing his gold cigarette case and that maybe one of our maids was a thief. He did so more to warn me than with any great desire to recover the case. I brought in a plainclothes man, who secretly searched the house. The case turned up in one of Tommy's socks. When I faced him with it, he offered no defense. He simply admitted the theft and said he had no idea why he'd done it. He was as calm and direct as George

Washington over the cherry tree. The trouble was that my detective found a lot of hacked cherry trees. I told the boy that if he did it again I would strap his behind with a belt till the blood ran. He didn't flinch. He said he would deserve it. I then ordered him to submit to something even harder. I told him to go downtown with me and give the case back to my partner with a full confession. And do you know he did it? And so handsomely that Ralph Sanderson has been his friend and champion in the firm to this day? Or should I say until yesterday?"

Orlando's voice was steady as he told the tale. He had obviously had years to assess the facts, to accept them as an integral portion of his domestic life.

"And Zoe knew all this?"

"Every bit of it. She was even more concerned than I. She wanted to send Tommy to a psychiatrist, but for some reason I was always convinced that would do no good. I had this curious idea that Tommy was peculiarly my task, my burden, if you will. Perhaps even my purgatory. As if some god or devil were saying: 'You think you're pretty hot stuff, don't you, Hatch? You think you can handle the world? Well, *here's* one for you!' "

I continued to sit there, silent and still, taking in something that was almost as novel to me as the news of Tommy's crime: Orlando was talking about his innermost self for the first time in all the years of our friendship. At last I ventured a comment.

"And it being your task, you didn't mind taking responsibility for it?"

"That's it. That's just it. Zoe was distressed by my attitude. She even hinted that there might be a touch of arrogance in it. That instead of playing the man tried by the gods, I was playing a god myself. But she went along. She warned me, but she went along. And when she goes along, you know, she never does it halfway. She never says, 'I told you so.' She's a partner in the adopted course, and she accepts full responsibility. Even this morning when I broke the news to her, she didn't reproach me for a second."

"But she took it hard."

"Less so than I would have thought possible. She was more upset, I'm afraid, about me than about Tommy. She said a strange thing. She said, 'You poor old darling, he's got you at last.'"

I frowned. "That's a bit Freudian for me."

"But I think Zoe was always afraid that Tommy was harboring revenge for something I did to him when he was at Harvard. He was expelled from a club there for cheating at cards. It was kept a secret. How I don't know. I guess Tommy's friends were more gentlemanly than he was. There were three of them who caught him and they gave him the option of resigning from the club or being exposed. He was allowed to use the excuse that the club had been distracting him from his work and that *I* had made him give it up."

"He told you that?"

"No, the father of one of his friends did. He joshed me with being so stern a taskmaster. I went right up to Cambridge to get the true story. Tommy made a clean breast of it. I told him, 'Cheating at cards when you play for money is the same thing as stealing. You know what I said I'd do if you stole again?' He didn't bat an eye. 'Go to it, Dad. I'm ready.' And right there, in his room, this odd scene took place. A grown man and a big husk — he was twenty at the time — he dropped his pants and underpants and leaned over while I whipped his bare ass till it was pink."

I will admit, the imagined scene transfixed me. It was at least a minute before I could say, "And then?"

"He straightened up, pulled up his pants, and we shook hands. 'Thank you, Dad,' he said. 'I knew you wouldn't say anything banal like this is hurting me more than it does you.'"

"Were there any more episodes? I mean, until now?"

"Not that I know of. But you can imagine how I watched him! He had no choice but to go into a firm where I could keep a daily eye on him. Because, you see, I was absolutely convinced that there *would* be another episode if I didn't. There was something in Tommy's very straightforwardness that seemed to point to a compulsion within him that he knew he could never control. He had *wanted* me to punish him! And if he had wanted that, didn't he want me to save him from doing it again?"

If Orlando could be such a realist in the family crisis, surely I, detached from it, could be. At any rate, I tried. "But Zoe felt otherwise? She felt that Tommy's jealousy of your success and the hopelessness of his ever even approaching it, created the compulsion, presumably subconscious, to bring you down? Or at least to hurt you as badly as he could?"

"Something like that."

"But you didn't think there was anything in that?"

"I wouldn't be so arbitrary. I wouldn't have the presumption to be the judge of what goes on in poor Tommy's psyche. And I'm perfectly aware that all the world will say I ruined him by keeping him on so short a leash." He rose now to walk to the window and gaze with unseeing eyes over the harbor. "Of course, it doesn't matter what they say. It only matters what I say to myself. And to one old friend." He turned back to me with the serenity of a man who is about to dismiss his visitor and go on with the work that he knows he will continue to do as long as he retains his health and strength. "And that is this. That the thing I'm most proud of in my life is to have kept Tommy out of the hands of the law for as long as I have."

Althea and Adrian

I HAD BEEN READING Althea Sartoris's short stories as they appeared in the *New Yorker, Harper's,* and *Harper's Bazaar* for two years before I met her in the winter of 1950. And I met her then because I asked my host at a literary cocktail party to introduce me. I was a newcomer to the world of books, having published a lacquered but popular whodunit, drawing heavily on my legal background, and I regarded Althea Sartoris as already a denizen of Parnassus. Her words, to use a hackneyed image but one that clings to the mind, were like jewels carefully laid out on a piece of black velvet, but with this difference: that when strung, as for the necklace or bracelet of a tale, they were united by a thread of common, even banal, expressions, such as would be used by her characters. Her art offered me a unique aesthetic experience: even such old clichés as "mad as a hatter" or "queer as Dick's hatband" acquired a new vigor when interwoven with such words as "hyaline," "hodiernal," "Procrustean." How did she do it? Well, you'll have to read her.

Of course there were those who found her precious and tricky, who maintained that her style was only fireworks to conceal a basic lack of content. There were others who accused her of capitalizing shamelessly on her Southern background (then very much in vogue) and even a small mean group that hinted that she did not hail, as the book jacket of her collected stories implied, from a Georgian plantation manor with Corinthian columns, but from a milieu closer to that of poor white trash. But despite all of these, her reputation in the "establishment" was high, and no one could take from her that she was the widow of Joel Prior, the young North Carolina novelist and fellow townsman of Thomas Wolfe, whose single novel, *Castle of Enchantment,* an epic of the American nightmare inspired by the fantasies and illusions that had gone into the building of George Vanderbilt's monstrous palace in the Blue Ridge wilderness, has become a modern classic.

She was sitting, for the moment anyway, alone on a settee, chewing the temple of her glasses, her eyes gazing abstractedly across the room. She seemed unaware of the party, and I noted that the whiskey in her glass was straight and iceless. "But she's actually pretty!" was my first surprised reaction. When she turned her head to look up at me, however, I could see that she was less so. Her eyes, a clear greenish-blue, seemed to ask what I wanted; they stared out at me from a pale, faintly ravaged countenance. Her red hair was drawn straight back to a knot.

"I had to take advantage of your momentary isolation

to tell you how much I enjoyed *The Castalian Spring*."

She murmured something inaudible but apparently pleasant, and I sat down beside her to suggest a motive for the enigmatic behavior of one of the characters in her story. She listened rather blankly, but not impolitely, until I had finished.

"Did you intend anything like that?" I asked. "Or am I way off the mark?"

"Something like that."

Her voice was low and soft, her articulation precise. She dismissed the subject, but not at all rudely. She seemed to imply that I had said all that was worth saying on the subject, and that she, at any rate, had nothing to add to it. Then she asked abruptly, but with decidedly greater interest, "Have you ever had pinkeye?"

"Hasn't everyone?"

"I was just wondering if I mightn't be developing a case."

She held up the eyelid of her left eye while I carefully moved the lamp on the nearby table so as to have a better look. I asked her to turn her head first left and then right. I peered through a small magnifying glass that I sometimes use in reading the telephone book, and when I pronounced that I could detect no evidence of inflammation, she was spontaneously and warmly grateful.

"You did that so conscientiously. You're not a doctor, are you?"

When I admitted to being a lawyer, she at once proceeded to ask me about a legal problem. Did the recipient of a letter have the right to publish it without the consent of the letter writer? One of hers, it appeared, had just been printed in an article about Joel Prior. I told her that she had a cause of action, but that, the letter being, as she admitted, innocuous, her damages would be nominal.

"How wonderful to know such things!" she exclaimed. "Most of my friends make very little sense except when they're talking about themselves, and then they're so boring you don't care."

I asked her what she had felt in her eye, and she described an itch that she had had or thought she had had. It had been "not so much a tickle as a brush, like that of a feather, as if something very tiny, but still alive, had been trying to get in under the lid and pull it down over itself and perhaps go to sleep there." She was absolutely serious. Althea, I was to learn, was that rarest of hypochondriacs, one who could talk interestingly about her health. But then her symptoms were always bizarre.

At this point we were joined by a man who had to be a friend of Althea's, for he did not address her. He reached out his hand instead to me with a quaintly ceremonious bow.

"I'm Adrian Schmuck. Yes, I'm afraid you heard correctly." He repeated his surname with a rough emphasis. "A pity, isn't it? And you're . . . ? Oh, Ruggles, of course."

"Mr. Ruggles is an attorney," Althea informed him, as one might, in a polite assemblage of the faithful, warn a friend that a heretic was present.

"He is also a competent practitioner of the novel form. I recommend to you, my dear, his *Murder by Merger*."

I think from that moment I regarded Adrian as one of my dearest friends.

He had long, lanky hair of a light dirty-brown color, a tall, gawky figure, and an oblong face that cascaded down into a prominent chin, which somehow managed to give a character at least of stubbornness to the whole. He stared at me for an uncomfortably protracted period after his initial compliment — I found out later that this stare was habitual, as was his way of thrusting himself too close to his interlocutor. He seemed to be trying to give one a fair chance to prove oneself not quite so ridiculous as his fixed half smile proclaimed. Was it a smile, or had his muscles finally frozen that way in his despair of finding sense in the world? But his manners were beyond reproach.

"I came over, dear Althea, to supply you with two more names. Let me elucidate, Mr. Ruggles." He turned to me with a grave courtesy that it would have been churlish to call false. Why then was I tempted to? "I'm afraid we're addicted to the low sport of the parlor game. We were fabricating names at last night's party and capping each other's titles. The subject was nighteries. With my customary staircase wit, I came up too late with the perfect name for our sailors' bar: 'The Arm Pit.' "

Althea clapped her hands with an enthusiasm that seemed to me undue. "Oh, Adrian, that's just it! And I thought of one for our elegant, post-theater spot."

"What?"

" 'The Koh-i-noor.' "

"That wins! It even beats my addition to our merchant fleet." He paused to give me a moment to savor their wit. " 'The American Dentist.' "

He and Althea exploded in obviously spontaneous laughter. It all seemed to me rather precious, but feeling that Althea was indeed the supreme literary artist of the mot juste, I could not but deem myself privileged to be present at the atelier of her composition.

My examination of Althea's eyeball seemed to have brought about my acceptance by her and Adrian, for in the next two hours the three of us sat in seeming content in our corner, discussing life and letters over constantly replenished drinks. Althea, I noted, had a remarkable capacity, for she drank her bourbon straight without interruption or apparent effect. Her condemnations of the artists and writers we talked about were sweeping, always launched in short, emphatic sentences, accompanied by snickers that seemed to take one's agreement for granted. And she had indeed a way of almost carrying one along with her. For example, when she came to the Broadway of my college years, which I had regarded as a kind of golden age, she made me suddenly see it in her light. Come to think of it, I reflected in dismay, perhaps Katherine Cornell's famous ringing tones *had* been synthetically noble, sentimentally clarion. And surely there had been something "stagy" about Lynn Fontanne and "cute" about Helen Hayes. But as her comments spread to cover beloved areas of fiction and poetry, it began to seem to me that I was giving up my idols one by one and that in time she and I would be left alone "as on a darkling plain" and that then I would see that pale smiling stare direct itself in my direction for a final annihilation. But we would not be quite alone. There would always be Adrian Schmuck.

"If Lynn Fontanne was stagy," he observed, "it was because she knew she was always on the stage. She had a way of fixing those dark eyes on her audience and seeming to drawl, 'Well, my darling boobs, did you think for a minute this *wasn't* a play? Isn't everything?'"

He rarely agreed or disagreed with Althea; he would simply offer his own novel opinion. One figure, however, was exempt from the criticisms of both: Althea's late husband. Indeed, they referred to the recent article of a well-known critic, which professed to reevaluate Joel Prior downward, in hushed tones, as if citing some ultimate apostasy. I had admired *Castle of Enchantment*, but not quite as much as they, so I kept my silence. Our session was broken up only when Althea, having exhibited no previous signs of inebriation beside the faintest stutter, suddenly clapped a hand to her lips and made a hurried dash across the room to a door that led to the bathroom.

Adrian seemed quite unperturbed. When I asked him if she was all right, he replied that it was a common occurrence. "So much better than getting drunk and disorderly," he murmured approvingly. "In a little while she'll come back, fresh as a daisy, as if nothing had happened."

"But why must she drink so much?"

"Isn't that the invariable characteristic of the better

American writer? And don't give me Emily Dickinson, please. I'm sure she had a bottle stashed away under her pillow."

"Did Prior drink?"

"Like the proverbial fish. And he had depressions, too. Black ones. In the last one he did himself in."

"And she worshiped him?"

Adrian looked at me as if I had expressed a new and interesting idea. "Was that it, do you suppose? He had the things she wanted, anyway. The genius. The looks. The lineage. With Althea, never forget the lineage."

"You mean she's a snob?"

He looked pained at my crudeness. "Let us rather put it that she doesn't find her own background sufficiently decorative. It doesn't go with her style. It was a mistake on God's part. Poor taste, really. Joel was a collateral descendant of the famous warmonger, Roger Prior. The one who pulled out his silk handkerchief as he harangued the Charleston mob and cried, 'Let us fire on Fort Sumter, and with this handkerchief I'll mop up all the blood that's spilt!' *That* is the kind of gesture our Althea loves."

"You say she wants his genius. But doesn't she have her own?"

"Undoubtedly. But of a different kind. She couldn't write a long prose-poem novel like his. Or at least she shouldn't."

"But she wants to?"

"Well, we all have our pet illusions. You must help me talk her out of it."

"Why should she listen to me? A Wall Street lawyer. Isn't that anathema to her world?"

"Her world? What is that? She likes law and order. Perhaps because there's so little of it in her personal life."

At this point Althea returned and, as he had said she would, resumed the discussion as if nothing had happened. She might not have been quite as fresh as a daisy, but one would not have imagined that she had just been violently sick to her stomach.

Adrian was right about her liking lawyers; at least she showed no aversion to me. I sent her a copy of my novel — which she had asked for, I had thought, in mere politeness — and she not only read it but wrote me an appreciative and perceptive letter. I was dazzled, and even more so when she proposed me as a member of a book class to which she and Adrian belonged, entitled, jocosely, the Better Wheaties, after a then popular brand of cereal. It met biweekly and consisted of junior editors of respectable publishing firms, a few aspiring literary agents, some conservative free-lance writers, and a sprinkling of amiable amateurs of the arts. The atmosphere was serious, intelligent, but not exciting. Althea was the undisputed star; they would all be very quiet when she offered, always in low tones, her emphatic opinions.

The contrast to one of her own parties to which I was invited was marked. She had a small apartment on Bond

Street with a good-sized living room, sparsely but neatly furnished and always seemingly freshly painted, where her more dedicated and much noisier literary friends foregathered to talk and drink right through the night. Althea, sometime in the early morning, would quietly pass out, and Adrian, with the help of another guest, would carry her to her bedroom, put a cover over her, turn out the light, and return to the party, which went on as if nothing had happened.

When I referred once in surprise to a taste so eclectic as to include these gatherings with the more decorous ones of the Better Wheaties, Adrian explained: "Jekyll-Hyde, wouldn't you say? Althea loves to be the oversized batrachian in the antiseptic pool of the Wheaties, but she's far too smart not to know who her real peers are. So she's drawn ineluctably to the big dirty pond and passes out because she can't stand all the racket that reminds her of the background she left behind in the Georgia hills. Think how neat her apartment is. That's her defense. Like her art, it makes her a 'lady.' "

I was a bit shocked by the meanness of his smirk as he pronounced the last word. "Then her liking the Wall Street lawyer is not exactly a compliment?"

"Oh, no," he responded cheerfully. "Any more than her liking *me*. If she does like me, that is."

Until then I had rather assumed that he and Althea were lovers, but he assured me that this was not the case. Indeed, with an upward roll of his eyes he thanked whatever gods there might be that he was not tossing *dans cette galère.* "I simply look after her," he elaborated. "That's what I *do,* you see. I look after people. Don't worry. I shan't look after you."

This was evidently no compliment. If Adrian was going to look after you, it meant that you were gifted. I never did find out what his private life was; perhaps he had none. He liked to describe himself as "neuter." Friendship, at any rate, with both sexes was his specialty, and he crossed many social lines of urban life. Not only did he know artists and writers; he was at home in the fashionable world east of Central Park and was in much demand at bridge parties, which provided him, he only half jokingly claimed, with a goodly portion of his income.

"Adrian's like a compulsive stripper," Althea, who loved to deride him, even to his face, observed. "But instead of taking off his clothes in public to shiver rapturously before a leering mob, he likes to exhibit his poverty to mammon." Here she shook as with some private ecstasy. "Can't you just see him at the card table with three diamond-studded dowagers, purring to himself, "Just *think!* They each have a million a year, and I have *nothing!*"

Adrian always took her cracks with equanimity. He may have taken pride at being, like Falstaff, the cause that wit was in others. For despite an incisive intelligence and reputedly perfect taste, he had never, I learned, produced even a critical essay, much less a work of art, or, so far as anyone could tell, attempted one. He seemed to live in order to delight his eyes and ears. He had had, for many years, a small regular job with the Red Cross at which he was supposed to work faithfully. Life commenced, presumably, when he left his office.

I began at last to suspect that the antagonism which Althea so often manifested to this constant companion was not the mask of friendship or even of dependency. Why then did she suffer him to be with her so often? Of course, he was convenient in fetching cabs and paying for them (neither Althea nor her late husband had ever saved a dime), in acting as host at cafeterias, and in providing more nurselike services. He was, one might say, more an amah than a friend. And what was there in it for him? Did he fancy himself a kind of Svengali who made his Trilby sing?

One day he came to a meeting of the Better Wheaties without her. To my inquiry if she was ill, he responded with a deep sigh.

"Much worse! She's in love. I think she's bringing him this afternoon."

"Shall we like him?"

"Can one?"

Well, some of us could. "Jeeks" Cram was not nearly as bad as the caustic Adrian had implied. He was certainly the latter's opposite, as much so as "tall, dark, and handsome" could be, and his handshake was as strong and his greeting as hearty as Adrian's were flabby and casual. He was a publisher, but of the business rather than the literary sort; he made no bones about his interest in big sales, and he let it be known that his forte was bringing "literature," as opposed to "books," to the wider public. "It's America's favorite fallacy that only trash will sell," he asserted.

Althea, clinging to his arm, aped the ingenue with a kind of lugubrious success. She somehow managed to look five years younger. When he went off to get her a drink, however, she came directly over to me.

"You'll like Jeeks," she murmured. "I'm sure you two will get on. He was a lawyer, you know, before he went into publishing."

I wondered if she assumed that all lawyers liked each other. "How does he get on with Adrian?"

"Oh, Adrian." She made a little face. "Not at all. He thinks Adrian's a bad influence. Jeeks wants me to try a novel. He says he can make it a best-seller. Of course, one never knows about that, but at least he's willing to try. He says I haven't begun to develop the real talent I have." She laughed as if to make fun of the idea, but I saw at once that I was not meant to join in her mirth. And she also saw why I was not joining. "Oh, I know, you think I've succumbed to flattery, and of course I have. The more outrageous it is, the better. Don't you just love it?"

When Jeeks came back with her drink, he took me aside in his turn, even though the reading was about to start. He led me into the vestibule, telling our hostess with a wave of his arm, as if he were one to whom all was permitted, to go ahead without him — he'd only be a minute. Outside he was a bit disingenuously frank.

"Althea tells me that you and I can talk freely, that

you're one of the few friends who understands her. Well, that little girl is going to need more pals like you, and I'm damn well going to see she gets them. Not this faded crowd of fags and dilettantes. She's far too good for them, as I'm sure you'll agree, just as she's far too good for the bunch of Reds she sees in the Village. I want her to have a life where she can become the great writer she ought to be. And that's the life she'll have after we're married."

"And when will that be?"

"Tomorrow, if she'll agree. Soon, anyway."

I shook his hand in a congratulation that could only be silent, and we went in to the reading of *Pierre*. I had no ear, however, for Melville's tale of incest. I found myself wondering if Althea had any loyalties at all, or if, chameleonlike, she changed her color whenever she deemed it suited her genius. I noted that afternoon that she appeared to be listening intently to the reading, leaning forward and resting her chin on her fist. But she made no comment when the passage was finished, nor did she so much as glance at Adrian, though he had stared at her throughout the session with his fixed half smile.

She did not ask him to her wedding reception, either. She and Jeeks, a divorcé, were married with only his immediate family present (she had none that anyone knew of) at the Municipal Building, but some fifty friends were asked to drink champagne with them afterward in the Library Suite of the St. Regis Hotel. Jeeks passed from group to group, as hearty as if it had been his bachelor's dinner, while Althea, strangely detached, acted more like a guest than a bride.

"Do you know what she just said to me?" she asked me, pointing quite obviously across the room to Jeeks's ample mother, an exuberant presence in silvery blue. "She said she couldn't wait for a wee grandson! He ought to be wee, all right. Don't you suppose Jeeks told her I'd had an early hysterectomy?"

"I don't think even he would dare."

"And then the father! He made a point of telling me that he trusted Jeeks to convert me from my 'Red' thinking! 'Red, Mr. Cram?' I asked. 'Well, didn't you vote for Truman?' he replied. Just like that! But I won't have to see much of them, will I? They live in New Jersey."

I decided that I could leave Althea to find out for herself the expectations of in-laws. I could only surmise that the late Joel Prior had been an orphan. "I don't see Adrian. Surely you asked him?"

"I certainly did not."

Even on such an occasion I could not help reproaching her. "Oh, Althea, was that kind?"

"Come over here, Dan. I want to talk to you about this."

She selected two chairs in a corner, so obviously apart from the group that it must have been evident to even the most forward that she did not wish to be disturbed. Had ever a bride behaved so? But Jeeks must have prepared his family and friends for her novel manners. Nobody attempted to join us.

"Adrian's been behaving very reprehensibly in my regard." Those clear eyes were now stern. When Althea pronounced judgment, her nervous habits dropped away. She might have been brandishing a pair of scales.

"He was so much against your marriage?"

"It's not that. All my friends were. They regard poor Jeeks as the most terrible philistine. Perhaps he is. I didn't pick him for his taste. But Adrian's been trying to undermine me in other ways. He's dead against this novel that Jeeks wants me to write — and that I *must* write, Dan!"

"Adrian wants you to go on with your short stories?"

"Yes! He drives me wild quoting what Henry James said to Ruth Draper, the monologuist, when she asked him if she shouldn't try acting in a play. 'My dear, you have woven your own little magic carpet. Stand on it!' "

"But I'm sure he means it in good faith. It's hardly a crime to advise you to stick to something you've proved yourself peerless at."

"It *is* a crime, when the motive is Adrian's. He wants to keep me down to small, perfect things. He even thinks my stories are now too long. He wants to cut and carve. To take out all but the most jewel-like sentence. What he really wants is to reduce me to an exquisite aphorist. A kind of latter-day La Rochefoucauld!"

"Well, I don't agree with him, of course, but I still don't see why that makes him an enemy."

"Because don't you see, Dan, what he's really after?" Her voice rose to meet the drama she was creating. "He wants me to be a nothing, a zilch, a cipher, like Adrian Schmuck. He loathes the creative world. He's simply eaten up, actually putrid with envy. He's a malevolent incubus, wandering through the world of art, looking for victims to reduce to his own hollow state. He's a vampire, that's what he is!"

"All right, all right!" I raised my hands to check the onslaught. "Cast him into outer darkness to weeping and gnashing of teeth. Let's get back to you and Jeeks. Where are you going to live after the honeymoon?"

"Well, in the first place it's going to be a *real* honeymoon. I've made Jeeks take a leave of absence of three months, and we're going on a cruise to the South Seas. Oh, the rest it will be! And if you *knew* how I needed it, Dan. We've picked a boat that's supposed to have no cruise director, no organized sports or social get-togethers, no razzle-dazzle. Long quiet days in a deck chair and tea with a quartet playing Strauss or Offenbach and nurse-like stewardesses to minister to your every need. Oh, we shall leave the hurly-burly way behind. And when we come back, no more glaring city life. Jeeks has agreed to commute, and I shall spend happy days in the lovely little house we've taken in Westchester, working a bit in my tiny garden and writing my beautiful, beautiful novel!"

What could I do but raise my glass and drink to her future?

When I told Adrian of her plans, he threw back his head and snorted. "I'd given it a year. Now I won't give it six months!"

Well, Althea's second marriage *did* last a year, but when it broke up it did so in a manner more sordid than even Adrian could have foretold. Once established in her dream house in Bedford Village, she not only resumed her heavy drinking, she started coming into the city without

Jeeks and was seen by various friends in some low dives in rather louche company. Finally, she did not return to Bedford, but moved in with a painter and his wife in the Village. Rumor could not decide which one was her lover. Or both?

Even the most radical of her old friends felt sorry for Jeeks. Yet when I lunched with him, at his invitation, he seemed more baffled than agonized. He might have been an Endymion ravished by a moon goddess. What had happened to him was not in the course of human events.

"When we had our last talk," he complained, "she looked at me as if I were a stranger. The place she's living in is almost a slum. And you know how trim she used to keep things! I don't know what her new friends are like — they had the decency not to be home when I came — but I suspect the worst. When I asked if she wanted a separation or a divorce, she simply shrugged and said, 'Whichever.' I talked about some sort of settlement, but she wouldn't take a penny. Not that I offered much, after the way she's behaved. But still, I don't want her to starve."

"Oh, she'll sell a story, never fear."

"She will if she writes one. But how can she do that if she's gassed half the time?"

"In the other half. A real writer always finds the time, and she's certainly that. I'm glad she won't take your money. At least that shows a remnant of style."

"What would you do then? Go ahead and divorce her?"

"What else? You owe her nothing. You must try to forget her and get on with your own life."

Which sensible advice he took — unless, as I suspect, he had already decided on that course. But Althea went from bad to worse. She quarreled with her painter and his wife and left them for a cheap hotel. She quarreled, it appeared, with most of her friends, about whom she then spread reckless slander. She did not quarrel with me, but then our paths no longer crossed.

One day Adrian called me at my office and asked me to come to his flat for a drink that evening. "You'll find an old friend of yours here." I guessed that it would be Althea. She seemed wonderfully pulled together and very much her old self, except that she was drinking iced tea in a tall glass, constantly replenished by our watchful host. She offered no explanations or apologies, but simply picked me up where she had left me. The three of us passed an agreeable hour, and I took my leave when she explained that she was on a new and rigid schedule and that Adrian was about to take her home. In bidding me good night she confided that she had given up her novel and had gone back to the short story. I approved.

I learned later what had happened. A month before, Althea had passed out on the street and been taken to Bellevue Hospital. There she had suffered a minor heart attack. Adrian had gone to see her, and she had been released in his custody. He had nursed her in his apartment until she was well enough to return to her hotel. Thereafter he had visited her daily to ensure that she was adequately fed and cared for, and he had somehow persuaded her to go on the wagon. Soon she was writing again.

In the year that followed I saw Althea infrequently, for

she made a point of seeing only people who didn't drink, and even though I offered to imbibe only iced tea in her presence, she insisted that she would be uncomfortably aware that I was making a sacrifice. She soon reestablished herself as a writer of short stories. Adrian, acting informally as her literary agent, peddled her work tirelessly to the editors of popular magazines and managed to persuade several of them that she could command a wider audience than she had previously enjoyed, particularly among women readers, with the result that her income was substantially increased. He has told me since that he never charged her a commission, and I believe him absolutely.

Nonetheless, there came a day when Althea accused him of embezzling her royalties and broke with him. She then spread her vilification of his good character throughout the literary world, where it was not always disbelieved.

When I asked Adrian how he could explain such unexampled treachery to a benefactor, he passed it off easily enough. "Oh, it's not really treachery, old boy. Althea sincerely believes that I robbed her. It's paranoia, pure and simple. It's always going to be Althea alone against the big, bad world."

"Except for Joel Prior?"

"But he's dead, don't you see? If I were to croak, she might canonize me, too. Face it, Dan. Our darling Althea has a wee bit of the monster in her."

"I think it's remarkable of you to be so detached. I'm afraid I can't be."

"But, you see, I'm not really detached at all. I'm a passionate admirer of her genius. It has been my entirely adequate reward to be able to feel that I've played some small role in its development."

"Your humility, then, is commendable."

"But I'm no more humble than I'm detached! Her genius is not Althea's private property. It's something, shall we say, more on loan. Anyone who nurtures it becomes a part of it. There's no more place for pride than there is for modesty."

I debated this for a moment. "Your relationship with her can't have always been quite that cool. Weren't you and Althea friends? Or didn't you think so? It's hard for me to imagine that you felt no sense of betrayal when she turned on you."

Adrian at this broke into a cackling laugh. "My dear fellow, I never even liked her!"

In the days that followed I found myself feeling almost sorry for Althea.

Guy Hallowell

In 1939 GUY HALLOWELL struck me as the happiest man in the world. He was still under fifty, in fine health, the husband of an amiable, adoring, and very rich wife and the nationally known editor of the letters and diaries of the antebellum Virginia statesman Murray Ogden, published in an endless succession of large handsome volumes under the auspices of the University of Virginia. And, as if all that were not enough, he was the proud owner of Ogden's Palladian villa, Planter's Grove, whose central red-brick square with its Doric white portico stretched its two long pavilions, like the wings of an albatross, on the crest of a hill overlooking Charlottesville. It was deemed by many the finest of the houses designed by Jefferson.

I was a law student at the university and not eligible to take the sole course that Guy taught at the college, but his wife was a cousin of my mother's, and I was invited frequently to Planter's Grove, where the Hallowells entertained the elect of the university and gentry of the surrounding countryside, plus a steady flow of house guests from fashionable New York and Boston. For neither Guy nor Molly was native to the state of their passionate adoption. Guy had been born a Bostonian and Molly a New Yorker, which gave to their gatherings a pleasant cosmopolitan flavor.

Molly was tall, thin, and quiet, with brown hair and complexion, only modestly good looking. She seemed to know at once what every guest wanted to eat or drink or talk about, and she moved easily and promptly to provide it. She was intelligent and amusing and always kind, but somehow muted. She had obviously adapted herself to her stronger and more colorful mate, though this appeared to have been wholly her choice. Mother used to say that she was making up to Guy for the fact that she had borne him no children, but this was typical of Mother, who always placed an undue value on babies, and anyway no one knew why the Hallowells were childless. Certainly, Guy didn't seem to mind it. He had the sense, unlike many of the blessed, to enjoy the myriad blessings he had.

I always think of him as the age he then was, and indeed he did remarkably maintain that appearance for the rest of his long life, reaping the compensation of one whose pale, bony countenance and premature gray hair had, as a youth, according to Mother, made him seem old. But maturity and fulfillment had brought him a more rounded face and sturdier figure without eliminating any of his intellectual air. Guy's pale blue eyes gazed at you from a long lineless face under a noble brow and thick crown of gray. They seemed to absorb your every word, though in fact I suspect they were a mask behind which he was already preparing his beautifully articulated response. Anyway, he heard you; he took in everything you said, even if his deeper concentration was naturally upon his own superior cerebrations, and if he laughed at your remarks or nodded in grave accord, depending on which reaction was appropriate, it was with a delightful and infectious gaiety or sympathy.

But stop. I see I have implied that he was an egoist. And he *was* an egoist. He was very keen indeed on Guy Hallowell and all his wonderful accomplishments. How could he not have been? So long as he never *said* so, so long as he heard you and appreciated you and laughed merrily with you when you were witty — or tried to be — why go burrowing behind that elegant façade to drag out evidence of that self-love that we all share and that many of us haven't the decency, as he had, to conceal? Well, the answer to that question will come later.

Certainly it was not asked by the friends who flocked to Planter's Grove. Guy had the knack of knowing how to appeal to academics as well as to socialites. The former could enjoy his fine wines and beautiful house and the grace of Hallowell entertaining, and feel excused for their dip into mammon by the indubitable value of Guy's scholarship. And the socialites could indulge the fantasy that their friendship with Guy might entitle them, just by itself, to a cozy little corner of academe. For could anyone deny that the multivolumed but ever continuing documentation of the life work of the great Virginian philosopher, wit, and "compromiser" was a monument in American letters? If Murray Ogden had been elected president instead of Polk in 1844, might the Civil War not have been averted? Oh, yes, how eagerly the New York friends, when the Hallowells came north for a visit, would hustle to the telephone to secure the choicest guests for a welcoming party, tossing out the not to be resisted bait, "Guy and Molly are coming."

Before Charlottesville I had known them only slightly, as my parents, between them, had hosts of cousins and tended to see more of those with children the same age as their own. But now I found myself a regular guest at the large Saturday night dinners at Planter's Grove. Certainly the Hallowells entertained with a lavishness rare among my relatives. Molly's fortune, of course, did not derive from our side of her family, but from her mother, Aunt Leona, an heiress of the Comstock Lode, and this was a fact that Guy was always glad to recognize. Indeed, I felt he rather overdid it one night when a young and newly appointed professor of English at the college put this inquiry to his host:

"I wonder, Mr. Hallowell, if you could tell us something about the financing of the Ogden papers. Surely the number of researchers employed, plus all the expensive printing and editing, is not in the scale of our other scholarly projects."

Guy smiled, as if delighted at this chance to give Molly

her due. "My considerably better half has been kind enough, trusting enough, and, may I boldly add, *wise* enough, to pick up the whole tab."

There was a scattering of appreciative applause, but Molly looked decidedly uncomfortable. She always shrank from any reference to her financial participation in Guy's work. And certainly, if she had any awareness of the reaction to it of my parents and many of her other relations, her discomfort would have been understandable. For it was characteristic of the New York milieu from which they sprang that they should never refer to the Ogden project without at once bracketing it to "Aunt Leona's money." It was not that they were unduly dollar-minded or even philistine; the reference was more in the nature of a pious muttering of a *deo gratias*, an automatic bow of the head in recognition of the source of all benefits. When I would protest that this habitual coupling of cash with Guy's work implied criticism of him as a profligate spender, or even a fortune hunter, and ask them if "Aunt Leona's money" would have been better spent on race horses or yachts, they had to deny it, but I still wondered if, deep down, they didn't regard my suggested alternatives as more appropriate to, more in keeping with, a mercantile fortune. The spending of it on scholarship might seem almost like covering it up, hiding it, even "laundering" it. And there was nothing to be laundered, was there, about Aunt Leona's millions?

On the other hand, in justice to my parents, I had to recognize that there was some warrant for their inevitable additional comment, on any mention of this topic, that it seemed a great deal of expense and labor to produce the complete edition of one man's literary remains, an adequate amount of which, for the vast majority of even cultivated readers, had already been published before Guy ever undertook his life mission. His Murray Ogden documents, by the time he was fifty, already totaled some thirty large beautifully bound green volumes issued to a list of private subscribers that included many of the great names of the planet. But I could and always would fall back on the argument that it must be worthwhile to do one thing perfectly.

There was one occasion, anyway, when Mother took my side, prompted to it by an unusually violent comment from Father about Guy having built himself a "cozy nest" with the golden twigs he had garnered from his mother-in-law's market portfolio.

"I really don't see why you have to go that far, Joe. There's no reason to suppose that Guy married Molly for anything but love, is there?" And when Father replied only with a skeptical shrug, she continued in a tarter tone: "Probably half the wives we know have as much, or even more money than their husbands. Do you imply that they were *all* married for mercenary reasons?"

"I'll bet it was a factor, anyway. In most of the cases."

"A factor? Then I suppose factors can work both ways?"

"How do you mean?"

"I mean for or against marrying a girl. You're so holy

about it, I suppose you wouldn't have married me if I'd been as rich as Molly."

"You're right. I wouldn't have. The money would have scared me off."

Mother really flared at this. "Then you married me for my poverty! Which I think is much worse! It's so small and smug."

They seemed on the verge of a real quarrel when Father diverted her attention by quoting the old saw that men who married for money usually earned it.

"You mean because heiresses are so spoiled and demanding? Well, that's certainly not Guy's case. Molly is the exception to prove that rule. She's been his slave. But I can't blame *him* for that. Women who turn themselves into carpets must expect to be trod on."

I did not agree that Molly was trod on. All the time I was in law school it seemed to me that Guy and she were the happy partners of a shared enterprise. Of course, he, as the scholar and originator of the project, took the lead, but Molly was certainly well read in antebellum civilization and seemed to take a lively if quiet interest in her husband's constantly repeated stories of Ogden and his times. Never did she appear in the least bored. She even took up the cause of Sophia Ogden, Murray's wife, and spent many of her leisure hours helping one of Guy's researchers in the editing of that good lady's own voluminous epistles.

"People are always joking about Guy's imagining that he *is* Murray Ogden," she told me one Sunday afternoon, when I had called and found her alone. "They like to point out that he uses Ogden's cane when he walks in the fields. Some have the gall to say that he's even beginning, when he thinks no one's watching, to simulate Ogden's limp. Of course, that's all perfect nonsense. It's true that he changed the wine closet when he found in a letter that Ogden had kept it in the west pavilion, but that was because it turned out to be a better place for it." And then she offered me her shy smile. "Still and all, Dan, if he ever *should* try to slip away from me in the guise of Murray, I shall be right after him in that of Sophia!"

We both laughed and the subject was dropped. But I had the feeling that she had taken advantage of Guy's absence to drop the hint that she was quite aware of how people talked about his obsession and to assure a young cousin, who might tell the others, that she had it firmly and pleasantly under control.

But did she? Already by the time that I graduated from law school, there were those who were less jocose about the development of Guy's identification with his hero. The witty phrases from Ogden's letters that used to adorn his conversation, always with a respectful attribution, now began to appear as if his own, and a faint Southern accent crept at times into his clipped anglicized syllables. He kept a series of huge albums in one of his workrooms which had a page for each day in Ogden's long life. He loved to take his visitors in there and ask them to pick a day.

"July 18, 1838," I once gave him.

Instantly alert, he rapidly turned the big pages of one of the tomes, flat before him on a long table. "Sorry," he said in a vexed tone. "Nothing on that day."

"July 19 then," I substituted, almost apologetically.

"Ah, that's better. Ogden rode over in the morning to Monticello to call on Uriah Levy, the new owner. That afternoon he wrote to one of Jefferson's Randolph grandsons in Richmond to describe the sorry state of the mansion and to ask if anything could be done about it. At night the Thomas Fairfaxes and Henry Bruen dined at Planter's Grove. And he records the death of an old slave, Sally."

Guy's passion for reassembling all the scattered original books and furnishings of Planter's Grove at almost any price would have placed him at the mercy of exorbitant dealers had his shrewd business sense not prompted him to make his purchases through agents. He came to believe that he had a kind of second sight in locating and identifying Ogden material and spoke to me quite complacently of the "friendly spirit" that had guided him to a chest of drawers in a Richmond antiquary which had turned out, unknown to the dealer, to have the Planter's Grove mark on one of its legs.

"Do you suppose it's Ogden's spirit that's helping you?"

"Oh, I don't make any such grand claim as that."

The smirk in his smile, which seemed to deny the denial, drove me to go on: "Of course, it might be he, but mightn't it also be the spirit of some dead would-be collector who is trying to accomplish through you what he couldn't afford to do in his lifetime?"

Guy obviously didn't care for this theory at all. "I should venture to suppose," he retorted, a bit stuffily, "that if there were a spiritual connection with the past of this house, it would be a more direct one than that."

The war broke out shortly after my graduation from law school, and during my four naval years I did not see Guy and Molly at all. He wrote me, however, long, wonderful letters. They were quite as good as, and rather like, Murray Ogden's, chatty, gossipy, vivid, shrewd, and with splendid aperçus of political and even military matters. I savored them aboard my landing ship in torrid atolls and on long, slow, inter-island ferrying, and I have kept them all to this day. I think Guy must have deemed it a war duty to entertain a serviceman, and he certainly succeeded with one. In the first years of renewed peace I was invited down to Planter's Grove for a long weekend every spring and fall, but it was not until the early 1950s that the old intimacy of my law school days was resumed.

This was occasioned by the death of the Hallowells' old lawyer and their decision to retain me in his place. They were, of course, residents of Charlottesville, but as Molly's securities and trusts were all handled by a New York bank, and as I was admitted to both the Virginia and New York bars, I seemed to fit their legal needs, with my added qualification, important at least to Guy, of having "something of a literary smell." They had a good deal more legal business than I had first supposed, with the management of Planter's Grove, the handling of the Ogden project, and the constant redrafting of their wills to implement their elaborate posthumous plans for an Ogden Foundation in the mansion, to be devoted to scholastic research, and I found myself, every year, making a number of agreeable visits to Virginia.

On one of these, quite by coincidence, I made an interesting discovery about Guy's "friendly spirit." It was just after my arrival, at lunch, when I noted a peculiar glint in his eye.

"Congratulations are in order, my dear Dan," he announced with his broadest smile. "You behold before you the happy owner of the Evansdale letters!"

Of course, by now I was enough of an Ogdenite to know what these were. The "Sage of Planter's Grove" had for two decades corresponded with Lord Evansdale, both while that peer was British envoy in Washington and after his recall. Guy owned all the earl's letters to Ogden, but Ogden's to him had been stubbornly retained through the years by his English descendants, who had resisted Guy's most extravagant offers.

"What happened? Did someone die?"

"Two! Two earls within a year of each other! Double death duties brought the noble family to its knees."

"They must have indeed offended your gods."

"No sarcasms, please. You must make allowance for an old collector's greed. Of course, I should not have been such a brute as to wish a tragedy like that on them."

"Oh, never!"

"But it's an ill wind, as they say. And besides, they

made me pay through the nose. Never mind that. The bells are ringing throughout Ogdenshire!"

"It's a collector's coup, I can see. But surely you always had photocopies of the letters?"

"I did, of course. But there's all the difference in the world between working with an original manuscript and a photograph."

I could not imagine what it was, but I knew better than to argue the point. "I suppose Ogden's spirit is more with you when you look at his actual pen marks."

"That's not for me to say."

"Has your 'friendly spirit,' as you call it, ever shown you things not connected with the Ogden papers?"

Guy looked up sharply. "What makes you ask that?"

"Nothing. It just occurred to me."

"It's curious that it should have. Something rather odd happened here a fortnight back."

"Please, Guy, must you tell Dan that?" There was a note of real uneasiness in Molly's sudden plea.

"Oh, my dear, it will *amuse* Dan. Now, please don't fuss." He turned back to me. "I was going to the room in the east pavilion where I keep the old newspaper files when I was suddenly struck with this thought: Don't go in there. Don't go in there, because there's a black man lying on the floor. A one-armed black man who is probably dead. Yet the thought caused me no particular agitation or fear. It was simply a fact. The room was not in a condition to be visited. So I went back to my library. And then I thought, How absurd. There can't be anything in that room. So I returned to the east pavilion and opened the door. And I was right. There was nothing there."

Guy paused, but only for dramatic effect.

"Only days later," he continued, "a letter of Ogden's turned up at a Swan auction in New York which I of course bought. It related this incident: Ogden had freed one of his best house slaves, a butler called Ralph, and obtained a job for him as a valet in Philadelphia. But after only a year in the North Ralph, traveling with his new boss, lost an arm in a railway accident, and, of course, as happened in those hard days, his job along with it. Ogden had taken him back in his old position despite the handicap. And then the unfortunate man had been murdered. By whom it was never discovered, but some suspicion fell on the man who had taken Ralph's place as butler and been sent back to the farm when Ralph returned. Apparently the other slaves had resented the reappearance of the emancipated one from the North. Anyway, no one was ever charged with the crime."

"It's a horrible story!" Molly exclaimed with a heat unusual for her. She had been twitching uneasily during the narration. "It's a horrible story, and Guy won't see why!"

"Murder is always horrible, my dear."

"It's not just the murder. It's the attitude of the other slaves. Their hatred for one who has got out of hell and come back!"

"Really, Molly. Hell? Haven't I shown you a thousand times that Ogden was the most benevolent master in all of Virginia?"

"But he was a master! He was like De Lawd in *The Green Pastures*. If they loved him, it was the way dogs love. For he'd turned them into dogs!"

Guy, with a pained expression, turned away to me, as if to divert my attention from her lapse of taste.

"Of course, Dan, my vision of the body in the newspaper file room, if vision it were, would not stand up in any investigation of second sight. And even if I were believed, it could always be argued that some earlier reader of that letter had told me about it and that I had simply forgotten."

"Except you would never have forgotten anything that related to Murray Ogden."

"No, my friend, I don't think I would have."

"Oh, I suppose you may have had your vision," Molly conceded in a tone that was almost impatient. "Enough crimes have been committed in this house to saturate its atmosphere."

Guy still tried to minimize this new antagonism. "Suppose what you say were true, my dear. You still shouldn't hold it against the beautiful old place. Even Nero's golden palace isn't to be blamed for the curious malfeasances of its builder."

"Unless the present occupant condones them."

This was my introduction to the rift between Guy and Molly on the subject of his hobby, which had so long seemed one of their strongest bonds. It grew in time until it began to spoil the pleasure of my visits. Molly would be her old pleasant, compliant self when subjects other than the old planter were being discussed, but when, inevitably, Ogden found his way into the conversation, she would frown and lapse into silence, or else make some dry remark or even leave the room. And I began to feel, particularly as Guy's researches reached Ogden's later years and the long correspondence with John C. Calhoun, that her attitude was more than connubial petulance or boredom, that it had some considerable justification.

For Ogden and his old die-hard South Carolina friend were as one in repudiating the earlier apologies of Jeffersonian slaveholders, who had urged their northern critics to await the natural demise of an economically doomed institution. Ogden now insisted that, on the contrary, the system was the only feasible way for blacks and whites to coexist. He was too loyal a Virginian, according to Guy, to be comfortable with a theory that rested his state's economy on a rotten plank and too much of a humanitarian to care to believe that he held his Negroes contrary to the will of God. In his letters to Calhoun, therefore, he poured forth the arguments that slavery was recognized in the Bible, that it provided a decent support for a still savage race, and that it looked after Negroes far better than capitalism did the factory workers in the North. What distressed me was that Guy, failing to see that a moral justification of slavery inevitably corrupted the whole moral code of which it was made a part, was beginning, in defending his hero's sincerity, to have to defend his code.

When I asked him once how Ogden handled the gruesome cruelties of the slave ships, he insisted vigorously that Ogden had always loathed the slave trade and had supported its prohibition.

"But by then the South had all the blacks it needed."

"What could Ogden do?" he demanded. "He was faced with a fait accompli. There were the blacks, millions of them. They could hardly be sent back. The past could not be undone. But it did not have to stain the present. As he wrote to Calhoun: 'The rape of the Sabine women was no derogation to the peaceful and honorable marriages that resulted from it.' And as little, he believed, should the cruelty of the slave trade taint the present relations between master and slave on the great plantations."

"I don't suppose there were many peaceful and honorable marriages between those masters and slaves," Molly put in dryly.

"But how could there have been, my dear? It would have been against the law as well as against their moral code."

"Would it have been against *your* moral code, Guy? Would you have even looked at me had I been black?"

"My darling girl, I would have loved you had you been all the colors of the rainbow!"

Well, that was better, of course, but how far did it get them?

That Molly was now actively alarmed at the intensification of Guy's identification with Ogden was made tragically clear to me when she came to my office without him one morning during their annual winter visit to New

York, where they always occupied the same suite in the St. Regis. She looked very pale and unwell, nor did she offer me so much as a smile.

"Guy doesn't know I'm here. There are times, I suppose, in every marriage when one spouse must act alone. I have decided to change my will to direct the sale of Planter's Grove on my death. I am convinced that it would not be healthy for Guy to live there alone."

I was silently astonished for a moment. "You really believe, then, that he is affected by some spirit in the place?"

"I don't know what it is that affects him. Whether there is some ghost of Ogden there, or ghosts of old slaves, or whether it's just Guy's imagination or mania or whatever. All that matters to me is that he is less and less himself in that house. So long as I'm alive, I can fight it. But when I'm gone, I want him out of there. I shan't tell him, because there's no point hurting him before it's absolutely necessary. He'll learn soon enough, anyway."

"Molly, what are you talking about? You're a good seven years younger than Guy."

She paused, looking down at my desk top. "I guess you'd better know, Dan. My lawyer should. I have a serious heart condition. I could go anytime." She must have been shocked by the depth of dismay in my eyes, for she put up both hands as if to ward something off. "Please, Dan, no sympathy! I can't cope with that and the business at hand. I've been to every doctor. There's nothing more that can be done. So let's get on with the will, shall we? It's going to take enough time as it is, and I don't know how much I've got. All right? Will you be a good boy?"

What other kind of boy, under these circumstances, could I be? I closed my eyes for a moment while I pulled myself together. "Of course, Guy could always buy the house in," I pointed out.

"Precisely." Her tone showed relief at how I was taking it. "Which is why I want to leave it to the university with a large cash bequest on condition they accept it and take it over as soon as practical after my death. Guy will have plenty of money to buy any other house in Virginia that he wants."

"But not one of Murray Ogden's."

"No, thank God, there's only one of *them*."

We got right down to details. Molly had thought it all out. I was to go down to Charlottesville to obtain the consent and agreement of the university, which should not prove difficult, as it had long had its eye on Planter's Grove as a cultural center and site for official entertaining, and had even solicited its devise from the Hallowells. The posthumous foundation of Guy's dreams would have to be located in another mansion, but Albemarle County was fortunately full of them. It should not take too much time to implement Molly's plan.

Alas, it took more than we had. Molly died, as she had foreseen, very suddenly, only weeks after our interview, while the new will was still in draft. Guy, who had been aware of her heart trouble but not of its gravity, was utterly prostrated. After the funeral he interred himself in an Episcopal retreat and communicated with nobody, even with myself on estate matters, for a month. My parents feared for his sanity.

I was married now, and when I told Alice of my decision not to tell Guy of Molly's aborted testamentary scheme, she thoroughly agreed.

"My only doubt," I added, "was whether I owed it to Molly's spirit to tell him how deeply the idea of his staying on in Planter's Grove had worried her."

"Because you think there really *might* be some malign influence there?"

"You think that's nonsense? You think it was all as much her obsession as his?"

"Why not? Haven't they lived there together, cheek by jowl, immersed in Ogdeniana, for thirty years?"

Molly's earlier will was duly admitted to probate, and Guy became the undisputed owner of Murray Ogden's ancestral acres.

I had reckoned, however, without Guy's suspicious nature. When he took up his normal routine again, which he did with more aplomb than any of his friends had expected — they had underestimated his absolute confidence in Molly's continuing spiritual presence — he put this question to me:

"I know, Dan, that Molly went to your office last winter without me. It so happened that I wanted to get hold of her that morning, and the man at the hotel desk gave me the number she had left where she could be reached. It was yours. Naturally, I did not call her there. It was none of my business. But now that I am her executor and sole legatee, now that I stand, so to speak, in her shoes, it is incumbent upon me to be aware of all her intentions so that I may properly carry them out. Was she planning a new will, which her death interrupted?"

What could I tell him but the truth? Was it for me to falsify a record between a couple as deeply united as they had been? He took my account like a man. Perhaps it had not come as a total surprise. He rose and crossed his arms solemnly over his chest.

"Her will be done. It is sacred to me. I will not deny that it will be a terrible wrench — giving up the idea of a foundation in Ogden's own house."

I might have been reconciled to this new chapter in the history of the Ogden papers had I not, fifteen minutes later, been startled, on my way out to lunch, to see him still sitting on a sofa in our reception hall. He was gazing across the room, a look of appalling sadness on his face. I hesitated to intrude upon his isolation, but he saw me and jumped up, at once his old self again.

"Ah, my dear fellow, forgive me for using your hall as a rest area. I'm lunching at the Downtown Association with an old classmate, and I had a few minutes to kill. Shall we go out together?"

It was Alice's suggestion, when I told her that night, that I delay the sale of Planter's Grove, on the excuse of some estate administration problem ("And don't tell me you can't find one of *them!*"), for as long a time as possible.

"Guy is never going to be happy away from that place,"

she reasoned. "Give Ogden's ghost the chance to work on him. Think of all the perfectly valid reasons Guy can bring to mind why he should *not* sell the house. How does he know that Molly didn't change her mind again before she died? If she'd really been so sure of what she wanted, wouldn't she have signed a new will right away and worked out the details with the university later? She knew how ill she was. Why would she take the chance?"

I had to admit that her reasons were cogent, and I had no trouble inducing Guy, whose conscience must have been satisfied with the resolution to sell, to postpone it for a year.

The passage of that year found him a changed man. He had entirely recovered himself and seemed almost as cheerful and charming as before Molly's death. I believe that he had canonized her in his mind and that her beatitude would no longer suffer the degradation of a too persistent mourning. I do not mean to make him sound cold, but there *is* a faint chill that emanates from true believers. Certainly this was the case on the day he came to my office to announce his new resolution to keep Planter's Grove for his lifetime.

"I have every confidence that Molly and I are acting as one in this decision. I want you to draw me a new will, going back to our old scheme of housing the foundation for the Ogden papers in the house. Planter's Grove in perpetuity! Oh, I know what you're going to tell me: that some day, in the far future, a wicked president of the university, aided and abetted by a wicked board of trustees, may find a way to topple my plan and turn the place over to developers. Well, that's why I have such a cracking good lawyer. I want you to draw the whole thing up so damn tight the evil ones will have a killing run for their money!"

When I ventured to inquire if he had had some guidance from the "friendly spirit," he made this cheerful reply:

"You can put it that way if you like. What I did discover was a letter of Sophia Ogden's indicating her belief in the ultimate manumission of the slaves. Let me quote it to you, *ipsissima verba*. She is speaking of the Compromise of 1850, and she says: 'I sometimes wonder, if I were a male resident in a territory about to be admitted to the Union, whether I might not vote to have it free and not slave. Think of all the headaches the issue has brought us!' So you see she was practically an abolitionist."

I tried not to smile. "And that, you surmise, would have altered Molly's thinking?"

"But of course! Molly and I will now be truly joint editors of the Ogden papers, or of the Murray *and Sophia* Ogden papers, as the project will be rechristened. I am instructing our people to reexamine every sheet of paper with so much as a note of Sophia's on it. Our research will show that between them the Ogdens covered every shade of opinion on the whole subject of slavery. Ogden and Sophia — Guy and Molly — two great teams!"

Alice clapped her hands when I told her that night.

"What a perfect solution! I'm beginning to believe in

that old ghost at Planter's Grove. And that he's a very clever one."

"But it's absurd! Turning poor Mrs. Ogden into Harriet Beecher Stowe. For that's what he'll do, you know. Once he feels that Molly's spiritual cooperation has been bought at this price, he'll be damned if he doesn't prove his point. Even if he has to forge something!"

Alice shrugged. "Who cares? He's only turning Mrs. Ogden into what she *should* have been."

"But what about history? Guy's whole life has been dedicated to discovering the absolute truth about one man. So much so that he has almost become that man. His million footnotes positively bristle with veracity. It's the only possible excuse for the whole gigantic labor. If the Ogden papers aren't fact, what in God's name are they?"

But Alice's second and final shrug was a clear indication that she did not consider my question even worth answering.

Clement Ludlow

IN 1955 I WAS STILL UNMARRIED and still an associate in Arnold & Degener and beginning to wonder how much longer I should remain in either state. My clerkship had been protracted by a three-year absence from the firm in pursuit of what I had come to regard, at least temporarily, as false literary gods, but now that I had been back in legal harness for the same period of time I was becoming uneasily aware that the day was approaching when I could be considered as "passed over" for partnership. Thus my assignment to a complicated estate tax case under Mr. Ludlow came as a happy omen. For it was customary, when a clerk was being considered for the ultimate promotion, to transfer him to a different department, that he might be examined by fresh eyes and his versatility tested. I had not previously worked for Mr. Ludlow, a shy and self-effacing man who nevertheless, because of the number and importance of his clients and his family connections (he was what was known as a "poor" Rockefeller, being the grandson of a sister of

John D.), occupied a high place in the councils of the firm.

He was fifty at this time and a supposedly confirmed bachelor, living with his widowed mother in a vast flat in one of the early apartment houses erected on Fifth Avenue to lure away the occupants of its moldering, high-maintenance mansions. His gentleness, equanimity, and mild formal good manners seemed appropriate to his slight, straight build and to the air of shadowy grayness on his grave, narrow, but still handsome face. His invariable kindness and consideration made him popular with the associates who worked for him, and he was almost idolized by the older female members of the staff, who found him "such a perfect gentleman." Yet he had the reputation of a man whom one knew little better after six months than one. As I saw more of him, however, I began to suspect that his natural reserve was only a partial cause for this. Too patient listeners are often not asked to listen. People are quick to assume that a placid demeanor and a regular life constitute a valid thermometer of the temperature within and that a man who is not anxious to tell you his secrets probably has none. But it was through coincidence and not owing to any insight of my own that I became the man in the office to know Clement best.

One evening, when he and I were still working after six o'clock, he asked me suddenly, "I say, Dan, if you've no plans for tonight, would you care to come home and have supper with Mother and me?"

Having heard so much about the Ludlows in the office, I was naturally curious to meet his mother and see how they lived, and we took a cab uptown to Fifth Avenue. The apartment must have required the services of three or four maids besides the old crone who let us in. Its rooms were very large, with tall windows looking down on Central Park. The dark furnishings and shadowy, ornately framed canvases had an air of missing the cluttered Beaux-Arts mansion from which they had been brought. Against white walls, with wide spaces between them, they seemed to shrink from too close an appraisal.

Mrs. Ludlow, however, was a person clearly indifferent to her physical surroundings. She was a tall, handsome old woman, with a high-pitched voice and precisely articulated phrases. One could imagine her, graceful and stately, posing for a portrait by Sargent, but in fact she was full of friendly nervous gestures, constantly clasping her hands or pressing them against her cheeks or even clapping them noiselessly to emphasize what she was saying.

"I'm always so happy to meet men from Clement's office. I think, had I been a man, I should have liked to be a lawyer. Lawyers are always so on top of things. I sometimes think, if all the world were lawyers, there would be no more wars, as everyone would see the other man's point of view."

I had little comment to make on an appraisal so unexpectedly flattering to my profession, and anyway Clement handled it with friendly mockery.

"Mother always sees the best in everyone, Dan. She thinks Judas only collected his thirty pieces of silver to put them in the plate on Sunday."

At dinner the conversation was largely between him

and his mother. It was curious to me that two persons who shared a domicile should have so much to say to each other. Clem seemed to delight in drawing her out, in showing her off, in laughing at her, but always as if she were something remarkable, precious, a piece to be displayed to a visitor who was honored in being afforded such a view.

Toward the end of our meal he evidently decided to spring a little surprise that he had been guarding for dessert, for he looked down the table at her with a rather foxy stare.

"What is it, Clement darling? Why do you look at me like that?"

"Don't 'darling' me. You've been at it again, haven't you? Did you really think I wouldn't find out?"

"Find out what? I haven't the faintest idea what you're talking about."

I began to wonder uneasily if it were possible that Clem was referring to some concealed minor vice of his parent, a habit of "nipping" in the afternoon, or even of taking some drug. It was obvious that Mrs. Ludlow was shamming and knew what he was hinting at.

"I'm afraid we're boring Mr. Ruggles," she said with dignity.

"You've been trying to break Grandma Knox's trust again. You've been vamping the trustees to get them to turn over the principal to you so you can give it away."

"And what, pray, gives you any such idea?"

"Joe Dobbin gave me such an idea."

"He had no business to do so!" Mrs. Ludlow tossed her head in a fine show of indignation. "It was a betrayal of professional confidence."

"It was nothing of the sort. He's not your lawyer. He's a trustee of the trust you were seeking to scatter to the four winds."

"You seem to forget, my darling child, that your grandmother established that trust for *my* benefit."

"And you seem to forget, my darling mother, that she gave you only a life estate."

"I didn't want *all* the principal," his mother replied with a sniff. "Only enough to buy one little summer camp for some poor city children. I can't see why you should object if God doesn't."

"Because even God can't break a trust drawn up by Arnold & Degener!"

Mrs. Ludlow turned to me with an apparent revision of her earlier opinion of lawyers. "Sometimes I think too much law and too single a life make my Clemmy just the tiniest bit hard. If he'd only get married! Are you married, Mr. Ruggles?"

"Not yet."

"But you mean to be, of course. You're still young. Sometimes I despair of Clemmy —"

"Please, Mother, you're embarrassing me!"

"I can't help it, my dear, I care too much. Do you know, Mr. Ruggles, he's had the blessed opportunity, three times a week, right here in this apartment, of meeting the most charming girl you can imagine — maybe not the prettiest, but an absolute darling — Ann Perry, a young teacher at Miss Bowden's Classes, who comes to read to me and sometimes stays to have supper with us. But will he do more than indulge in charming persiflage with her? No! And yet she finds him so delightful, so wise. She tells me she *likes* older men. I couldn't resist saying to her, 'Well, my dear, if you won't absolutely *kill* me for it, I'm going to give my boy the tiniest little hint of what you've just said —' "

"Mother!" Clem had jumped to his feet and was glaring down the table at her. "Mother, how *could* you? Must you always indulge your every whim? Have you no sense of shame?"

At this our little evening simply fell apart. Poor Mrs. Ludlow, crushed by what must have been an unprecedented outburst from so devoted a son, began to sob and wailed that no matter what she tried to do for her children, she was accused of tactlessness and extravagance. "I'm just a useless old idiot," she complained. Clem, appalled now at what he had done, did his best to apologize, but it was no good. I do not think that his mother was trying to punish him. I believe that she had too little vanity to realize how important a role she played in his life. She had had, after all, so many people in her own to love and be loved by — her son, her married daughters and grandchildren, and the host of her poor — that she could take love a bit for granted. Clem, I was beginning to suspect, had only her.

When she had retired at last to her chamber, and I

had suggested to Clem that it was high time for me to go, he seized me by the arm in agitation.

"You can't leave me now, Dan! I've got to have someone to talk to. You've heard so much, you might as well hear the rest. We can go to the library where no one will disturb us. I'll give you a nightcap. I have every kind of drink to offer you."

We had a lot more than a nightcap that night. In the cool, comfortable, leathery library, with its reassuring rows of standard sets, a bar table of glinting bottles and a crackling fire in the grate, I, at least, was perfectly comfortable. Clem, however, was very unlike the grave and sober partner for whom I worked downtown. I do not suppose he had many intimate friends, and the scene in the dining room must have created an agonizing need for explanation or even self-justification. He spoke in a tense monotone, pausing at times to stare at me with what seemed almost defiance, as though to demand if I presumed to censor him. I had ceased to be a clerk; I might have been a judge before whom he was pleading his case.

He told me that his celibate life had not been a matter of choice. He had simply been unable to establish a satisfactory relationship with a woman. Yet he had not accepted his fate passively. Too diffident to inquire among his acquaintance for the name of a skilled psychiatrist, he had consulted a lay analyst who had published an article in a popular magazine about a therapy he had used with alleged success in just such cases as Clem imagined his own to be. Myron Berger had recommended that the patient in daily life should do all the things he least liked to do.

"He started me out easily enough. He told me to cut down on my tips in taxis and restaurants, to measure them exactly to the service rendered. If a driver, for example, refused to turn off his radio, or to lower its blare, I was to give no tip at all and, worse, to explain to him the reason. And in a restaurant, even when I had guests, not to pay the bill until I had carefully checked each item and retotaled them. He made me walk into stationery stores and ask change for a ten-dollar bill without buying anything. When I introduced myself to someone at a party, I had to be sure that he or she got my name correctly. All this, of course, was by way of reducing inhibitions. And in time I graduated to even more embarrassing things. Oh, much more embarrassing! You may not believe it, Dan, but there came a day when Berger and I and his fat middle-aged secretary had a sandwich lunch in his office, all three stark naked! This was a giant step, he maintained, in annihilating what he called 'emotional constipation.' Of course, he and the secretary did not mind in the slightest. It was part of the regular therapy. But to me it was simple torture!"

The picture of Clement Ludlow under these conditions, with only a ham sandwich as a possible fig leaf, was indeed an appalling one. I could only maintain a sympathetic silence. The slightest comment might have shut him up completely, and it was obvious that he needed to talk.

"I quit my so-called therapy. I decided that the man was too phony. I was even ashamed of having stayed with him so long. And then in desperation I tried to make peace with myself and my single condition. What did it matter, after all, whether I ever loved or didn't love? Why did I always have to be comparing myself with other men? Did *they* care what I was? Of course not! They were perfectly willing to accept me for anything I wanted to appear to be. Oh, of course they might privately speculate that I was a neurotic virgin or a frustrated homosexual, but they didn't *care*. Nobody really gives much of a damn what another person is under the surface. So why should I? I decided to accept my life as it was. Order, peace, routine. My work. My clients and charities. Mother. The theater. Music. Books. A better life than most in this vale of tears."

At last I ventured a comment. "Much better."

He shook his head in silent demurral. "And then Ann Perry came here. A quiet little girl who didn't expect anything from anybody. Yet with a mind and a character of her own. And it suddenly seemed to me that she might be the answer I had been looking for! That I could offer her so many things she'd never had, money, security, devotion, travel, a good home, even children perhaps, and the total might make up for my emotional deficiencies. And I could guarantee that she'd never have to put up with bad temper or crankiness. I even dreamed that once we were together and relaxed, I might learn to love her as any young man might!" Here he clenched his fists, and

I wondered if those were tears that I seemed to make out in his eyes. "And then Mother comes smashing in to ruin everything! Making it so crudely obvious that she'd had the same idea. Making it seem like an act of purchase. Like a Jewish mama asking, 'Anyone know a nice girl for my Clemmy? How about you, Annie dear?' "

"But she's entirely right!" I exclaimed now, jumping to my feet.

He gaped. "What are you saying?"

"That your wonderful mother sees just what I see. That it's a marriage made in heaven!"

"But she's just wrecked it! Speaking to Ann like that!"

"Oh, Clem." I suddenly felt years older than this pathetically naive but still lovable man. "Don't you know that women don't *mind* that sort of thing? They're much tougher and more realistic than men."

"They are?"

"Of course they are. Go and call Miss Perry right now and ask her to marry you!"

"Now? At this hour?"

"Yes!"

He had turned very pale. "By God, I think I will." And he did.

The next time I was asked to dinner at the Ludlows' it was to meet Clem's fiancée. The engagement had not been announced, but Clem told me he wanted me to be one of the first to meet her. Only he and his mother and Ann were present.

I had expected, I confess, a kind of little brown wren who would lend herself to this Griselda role, and indeed Ann Perry was diminutive and brunette, with a plain but unobjectionable round face that one could imagine warming into something like prettiness under the right conditions, which Clem was presumably going to provide. But I had not been prepared, as one so often should be, for a character quite the opposite of what the scenario seemed to call for. Everything in her manner, the tilt of her chin, the stillness of her body, the pale composure of her features, suggested reservation. If the Ludlows had gained her, those clear brown eyes seemed clearly to imply, it was not by means of a large apartment or a lofty social position. This was again underlined by her failure to bow her head during Clem's uttered grace or to murmur the usual discreet Amen at its close.

"Dear Ann finds our little thanksgiving at meals a quaint survival," Mrs. Ludlow said sweetly, her sweetness untinged by the least reproach. "She is mindful, no doubt, of the millions who have less to be thankful for."

"It's not that, Mrs. Ludlow. It's more that I don't believe there's anyone up there to thank."

"Oh, I know you don't share our faith, my child. It's natural enough. Your life has not been an easy one. But I still can hope, when you and Clemmy are wed, that we may persuade you of some of the consolations of religion."

"I shall never try to convert you to my atheism, Mrs. Ludlow. Will you grant me like exemption from your Christianity?"

I looked down at my plate, embarrassed. A glance at

Clem showed me that he too felt the constraint. But his reaction was colored, no doubt, by some pride at the individuality of his affianced.

His mother, at any rate, took it in good part. "Oh, we won't be preachers, will we, Clemmy darling? We shall only hope that the example of our consolation may in time have its effect on dear Ann. That's one of the wonderful things about marriage." She turned to me. "You're not married yet, Mr. Ruggles? No, of course, you told me that. But you're still young. That's as it should be. Clemmy waited a long time, but it's a case of much better late than never."

"Hear, hear!" her son enthusiastically agreed.

"I'm not so sure of that." Ann's tone was reflective, almost impersonal, but the small smile with which she regarded her betrothed might have been meant to modify its seeming coolness. "Clement has spent a number of years creating the life of the perfect bachelor. His friends, his clients, his family, all dote and depend on him. His days are filled with good works, his evenings with dinner parties where he is always a welcome guest. He can travel to the places of his choice and see the things he wishes to see. Isn't it a precarious thing to add a new weight to a lovely mobile so delicately balanced?"

"Not if what is added is love!" Mrs. Ludlow exclaimed, clasping her long brown hands. "And that is what *you* will bring him, my dear. For without love, as Saint Paul said, one becomes as a noisy gong or a clanging cymbal."

"Ah, but that is the Revised Version, Mrs. Ludlow. To

a good atheist the Bible is literature, and as literature I can admit only the King James. And it is charity, of which Paul wrote to the Corinthians, not love."

"Love, charity, what's the difference?" Clem's mother equated them with a wave of her hand. "Put it, if you like, that it's charity you bring to my Clemmy."

"It might be more accurate to put it that I bring him the opportunity to be charitable."

"Ann, my dear!"

"It's all right, Mother. It's only Ann's way of having her little joke." He reached his hand down the table, and for an awful moment I was afraid she wouldn't take it. But when she did, it was with an almost feverish grasp.

What was her game? There could be no question of her welcome into the family by the effusive Mrs. Ludlow, no doubt of the devotion of her intended husband. Why then did she have to be so prickly? To underline her independence of the material advantages of the match? But if she wished to convince people that she was motivated by love alone, would it not be wiser to let a little more love be shown? Particularly if that was the case, which I suspected it was?

I was not invited to the party given by Mrs. Ludlow to make the official announcement of the engagement. This could have been easily explained on the ground that it was limited to a handful of relatives and partners, and that I was still only a clerk in the office. Yet I nonetheless found it odd. It seemed to me that Clem and I had achieved an intimacy that night that should have transcended such barriers. It even occurred to me that he might have become embarrassed by some of the things he had told me and did not wish to be reminded by my presence of what he now considered indiscretions. Did I recall too vividly that naked lunch in the therapist's office? Or had Ann taken a dislike to me?

The last hypothesis began to seem not improbable. I was already hearing some strange things about her from the older female staff members at the office. Of course, the ones who most adored Clem were quick to assume that she was a "little gold digger," and were anxious to pick up any dirt they could from the secretaries of the partners who saw the Ludlows socially. I was told that Clem's fiancée was very shy and silent, almost impossible to talk to at social gatherings, which came as no surprise. But what did surprise me was to hear that her manners were considered abrupt to the point of rudeness. It was said that she would hurry into the dining room as soon as she arrived at a dinner party and, if she found she was not seated by Clem, would switch the place cards. And that once at table she would make no effort to talk to the man on her other side, but would lean awkwardly over to eavesdrop on what her fiancé and his neighbor were saying. And that after dinner, as soon as the gentlemen joined the ladies in the drawing room, she would scurry over to sit by Clem and even hold his hand! It was generally believed that she was hysterically jealous, and people were already beginning to say that Clem had made a sad mistake to give up, at his age, his single state.

Clem, of course, had nothing to say about all this in the office, but I noted that she called him there several times a day, and that he would invariably talk to her, even when we were in conference with a client, and listen patiently, although sometimes with a look of constraint on his face, as she carried on at length, probably about the hour of his quitting work, for he always ended with the words, "Yes, dearest, I'll do my best to be there no later than six."

But all this was as nothing compared to what happened the first time I was asked to a party given in honor of the engaged couple by the Angus Degeners. He was the senior partner of the firm and had included some of the senior associates. I watched with considerable curiosity when Clem and Ann appeared. She seemed to have lost all her earlier assurance and looked very pale and suspicious, her eyes darting furtively around the crowded chamber. My host brought me over to meet her, murmuring as he did so, "I want you to talk to Miss Perry. She's supposed to be shy, but she may be less so with someone her own age."

I noted, sitting by her on the sofa, that she kept her eyes fixed on Clem across the room. I tried a humorous note. "Nobody's going to eat him."

She gave me a sharp glance. "I'm not so sure of that."

"But surely they're all your friends!"

"Mine? Are they? Are *you*?"

I was struck by how immediately she seemed able to make a reality of her nervous preoccupation. Whatever was troubling her made me imagine, as it evidently did her, that the faces around the room were the masks of a concealed hostility.

"Surely I'm a friend," I protested. "Didn't I show it the night we first met?"

"Because you sided with his mother? Oh, I knew about that. He told me about that."

"Then what more do you want?" I asked, bewildered. "I was all for the match."

"You were all for his getting married," she corrected me. "It didn't matter to you, or to anyone else, to whom. Except it might be better if it were someone meek and inoffensive. Someone who would look like a wife without asking too much. Why not Miss Perry? Exactly! *She* could be counted on to gobble the bait."

"My dear Miss Perry, I don't know what gives you such disagreeable suspicions. Surely everyone here wants to welcome you with open arms." At this moment I saw Clem's mother, followed by his two sisters and their husbands, making their rather regal entrance into the room as both Degeners hurried to greet them. "And how many American wives have the immediate and unqualified endorsement of their future mother-in-law?"

"Oh, I don't include her with the others."

"You don't?"

"No, no. Mrs. Ludlow has been perfect with me. She doesn't see people in frames. She only sees people."

I was beginning to be irritated. "Meaning she doesn't see you as someone she once employed?"

"Or as a poor little teacher. Or as someone twenty years younger than her son."

"What *does* she see?"

"She sees someone who loves her Clemmy."

Our host came over now, bringing a gentleman to introduce to her, and I crossed the room to sit by Mrs. Ludlow. It seemed to be an evening of frankness, so I told her what Ann had just said.

"Oh, it's quite true!" she exclaimed in her high, enthusiastic tone. "I see darling Annie as a creature shining with love. Clemmy is a very lucky man."

I ventured the opinion that it seemed a pity that her daughter-in-law to be did not take more pains to convey this impression to the rest of the world.

"You mean that she's *un peu farouche?* Perhaps just a touch, but that will pass as she and Clemmy settle into married life. She's so afraid, poor dear, that she's not good enough for him, and that his old world will somehow reabsorb him. Of course, that's perfectly ridiculous, and I tell her so. But Clemmy has to be the one to do it. He must learn to convince her of his love. He hasn't had much practice, poor boy, in that sort of thing. But he will get there. After all, it's the most natural thing in the world. As well as the most heavenly!"

I could not but wonder if Clem's love would survive the long period it might take him to learn to express it. "Perhaps they shouldn't go out quite so much until he learns," I was bold enough to suggest.

"But you see, my dear Mr. Ruggles, everyone *insists*

on meeting the bride to be. All of Clemmy's old friends and clients and cousins and members of his charitable boards. There seems to be no way out of it. And then, too, it doesn't do Clemmy any harm to have to adjust himself to another person's way of reacting to things. He's concentrated all his life on how *he* must behave to people, never on how they behave to him. And in getting engaged and marrying he's put all his energy into what *he* is feeling, into *his* love for Annie. That's really always been Clemmy's idea of his problem: learning to love, learning to give himself. It's only natural that the poor darling should have overlooked his real problem: which is *being* loved."

I was amazed, not only by the wonderful old lady's perspicacity, but by the calm way in which she accepted what she saw. "You don't think loving implies an acceptance of being loved?"

"Not a bit of it. Loving can be quite egotistical, I'm afraid. It is the acceptance of love that is generous. It's what turns love into true love."

I sighed. Perhaps she was right. But perhaps Clem, however much a child to her maternal eyes, was still too old to embark on this game. I did not, of course, express this apprehension to Mrs. Ludlow. But if I had, I am sure she would have simply clapped her hands and exclaimed that the game was what life was all about and that it was better to try late than not at all.

I was even less sure after the disaster of Ann's speech at the dinner table. Our host made a gracious toast to the engaged couple and then actually called on the future bride to tell the company how she liked finding herself a member of the "Arnold and Degener family." Clem jumped to his feet in too obvious dismay to protest that she was not used to speaking and that he would respond on her behalf, but to my astonishment and that of those who had met her before, Ann rose to address us in a level tone.

"It's all right, Clement, I'm glad to respond to Mr. Degener's inquiry. I have been welcomed warmly by everybody here tonight. As I have been welcomed on other occasions by others of Clement's friends and relations. What does it feel like, you ask? Well, I think I can tell you. I feel as if I were being warned as well as welcomed."

Here she was interrupted by laughter around the table. Everyone but me must have assumed that this would be followed by something facetious. Ann herself did not smile. She simply paused until silence returned.

"Warned that my shares in the stock company that owns Clement Ludlow do not represent a controlling interest. You see, I have already learned the language of your great firm, Mr. Degener. There may even be a question if my shares have a vote at all. Those of his partners have. They want forty percent of his waking hours and an even larger share of his thoughts. And there is his family. His sisters have no intention of releasing any rights in the devoted brother who has always been a helpful weekend guest, a valued adviser, and a loving godfather to their children. And there are the friends who will give up no part of the sympathetic ear that has so long reverberated with their multitudinous confidences. Only his mother has tendered me all her shares from the same open and sunlit heart that she has shown to her many charities. I drink to you, dear Mrs. Ludlow." Here she solemnly raised her glass to her Clem's mother, who smiled benignly back at her across the table as if it were the most normal of salutations. Then Ann glanced defiantly around the room. "And I am putting the rest of you on notice that I am a corporate raider who is going after the lion's share of Clement Ludlow and Company!"

Had she made her speech with even the hint of a smile, it could have been taken in questionable but not really bad taste. As it was, her tone simply stunned the company. Only when Mr. Degener rose to announce, "I think all brides feel that way, but very few have the guts to say it," was the situation partially saved. And then, suddenly, as if like a conductor he had raised his baton, those of the ladies who were socially adept turned to their neighbors and started talking rapidly on other subjects. There were no further speeches that night. But I shall never forget Clem's eyes. The pain they expressed was atrocious, and Ann's, staring at him, suddenly brimmed with tears.

Clem left the Degeners' party early, on the excuse of his mother's age, to take her and Ann home, but he asked me — or rather told me in a clipped whisper — to come to his apartment in an hour's time. When I arrived there I found him alone in the library, a very dark drink in hand.

"I'm terribly sorry, Dan, to keep you up so late, but you've been in this from the start, and you've got to help me now. Do I go through with it or don't I?"

As in that other evening in the same room, I thought it best to let him talk. He certainly went on. Indeed he was so upset as to be at times almost incoherent. His whole life, he told me, had been premised on his ability to get on with people, to hear their problems, to find their solutions, to assist them by the very impersonality of his sympathy, by acting as a calm voice from the dark silence of the confessional box.

"What is left of all that if Ann is going to wreck everything with her bluntness?"

"But the night I first met her she was very outspoken about being an atheist, and you didn't mind at all."

"But that was with Mother and you, who understood! I love it when she's outspoken with *me*. I've never minded what people said to *me*. But tonight at Angus's it was before my whole world. It was terrible, Dan, you know it was!"

"What was terrible?"

We both turned to face his mother, strangely gaunt in a long, inappropriately red wrapper, standing in the doorway.

"What was terrible?" she repeated in a harsher tone than I had thought she possessed. "To find that girl loves you? And doesn't want to share you with all the world? Isn't that what you've been yearning for all these years? Isn't that what you complained your life didn't have?"

Clem's face seemed to crumple. "You mean I've been a fool? And you've always known it?"

"No! I mean you're being a fool now. This is the life you wanted, my boy. Well, *live* it!"

He looked at her almost pleadingly. "And it will be worth it? You promise me?"

"It's certainly worth a chance."

Clem turned to me and smiled, rather foolishly, I thought. "Go home now, Dan. And bless you for coming and listening to my maudlin ravings."

I shook hands rather formally with the wrappered old lady who had suddenly become a hostess again.

"Good night, dear Mr. Ruggles. And sleep well!"

I hardly did that. I wondered most of the night how Clem would fare with his new resolution. But I was never to be sure, for he did not again refer to the doubts of that evening. Indeed, he hardly talked in the office or at our occasional lunches about Ann at all. By all reports, her manners, after their marriage, were somewhat improved. When they went to parties, at least, she no longer insisted on holding his hand. I do not know how she occupied her days (she had given up teaching), but Clem had a little volume of her poems privately printed and distributed to friends. A few of them were not at all bad. I supposed that she had now achieved her end as majority stock-holder in her husband's life and could relax her vigil. But whether Clem ever truly attained the goal of accepting her love, of which his mother had spoken so eloquently, or whether, if he did, it made up for the interruption of his old routine, I was not to learn. His demeanor had all the friendly gravity and impenetrability of earlier days. The Ludlows had no children, but one of Clem's sisters assured me that the sterility was not her brother's.

Abel Donner

HE WAS "MR. DONNER" to all the clerks and all but
the oldest partners. This was not because of autocracy on
his part; it was simply that the gravity and austerity of his
mien did not invite intimacy. He did his own thing, went
his own way, and presumably expected you to do the
same, though it was to be noted that he had his eye on
you more than you might think. Those expressionless,
unblinking gray orbs took in everything on which they
fell as he made his silent way through the long corridors
of Arnold & Degener, storing it away in his mind like a
computer. But if they noted something wrong, it was only
to the administrative partner that complaint would be
made. Abel Donner would have nothing to do with the
day-to-day running of his law firm, or with clients or matters not his own. He had always refused the rank of senior
partner, or even a seat on the committee of management,
yet his veto on any issue of policy, rendered only when
his advice had been sought, was accepted without dispute
by a firm that had developed a near total faith in his
wisdom.

I did not work with him until the early 1960s, when I was a junior partner; it was never his practice to deal with clerks. He treated me with the same dry, impersonal courtesy that he accorded to all in the office. If I made a mistake, he would never rebuke me, but simply sigh and murmur something about "these vexatious errors," as if the room were afflicted with flies or mosquitoes, a condition attributable more to fate than to myself. So long as he did not dismiss one from a case, one knew one was doing as well as could be expected.

He appalled me, but he also fascinated me. His philosophy, if such it could be called, seemed at every point the exact reverse of my own. I could not make out that he believed in anything but the application of the brace of law to the support of a fleshy boneless society that without it would have flowed idly over the ground like some viscous liquid. He would sit at his big desk in his long bare paneled chamber, staring sightlessly out the window as I expounded some problem I had encountered in my research, shaking his round bald head, reaching an impatient finger to scratch the gray fringes of his hair, twitching the little beak of a nose in the center of his lineless moon face, expressing with these few fretting gestures and the stiff stillness of the slight small body under the well-pressed dark suit his resigned frustration at the incomprehension of the world around him. And then, when I had finished, with a preparatory cough and a brief chewing of his slender lips, his sharp cackle of a voice would reply: "Well, well, let's see, let's see. Don't I seem to recall a city ordinance in 1932 that . . . ?"

And nine times out of ten it was just what I needed.

His clients were entitled, according to his credo, not merely to his best but to his all. He was indefatigable in his efforts to keep them, like some endangered species, safe in his preserve of legal propriety from the "poachers" of governmental law enforcement. Indeed he tended to regard any infraction of a code by a client as the fault of Abel Donner, for should he not have trained the client better? Yet this generosity of attitude was not extended to persons he did not represent. His whole humanity seemed confined to those who could afford his expensive counsel.

What did he do with the fruits of his labor? He probably hoarded them; he looked a bit like a miser in a Restoration comedy. He and his plain, dowdy, but darling old wife — she brimmed with a gentle if inarticulate good will — lived in a commodious Park Avenue apartment almost as bleak and bare as his office, and kept an old Cadillac limousine, but these appeared to be their sole luxuries. They gave no parties, had no country place (they went to a hotel in the White Mountains in August), and never traveled. A rigid and unvaried routine seemed to supply them with all the diversion they required.

But how could a man *live* in such dryness? He must have been like a camel in the desert with a hidden store of liquid. He had certainly no detectable interest in people or gossip or art or sports or houses or parties or books. If I spoke of any such things at his lunch club where he frequently took me while we were working together, I would get only a brief, blank stare, possibly accompanied by a shrug, to indicate that surely even *I* must see that such irrelevancies were not even amusing, and he would revert to one of the topics that filled his statistic-stored mind: the amalgamation of the city rapid transit lines or the creation of urban reservoirs. These dissertations took the form of monologues, and I had observed, at office parties, that a lawyer so addressed could be relieved by another, in sentry fashion, without Donner's appearing to notice the change in his audience. What it really boiled down to, it began to seem to me, was that he totally rejected the least bit of color or character or *feeling* in any subject presented. He was like Lawyer Crick in Henry James's *Ivory Tower*, whose whole person refused to figure "as a fact invidiously distinguishable" and who proclaimed at every pore "that there wasn't a difference, in all the world, between one thing and another."

And yet my description makes him sound colder than he was. There was more than a hint of kindness in his courtesy, and he even betrayed at times a closer acquaintance with the facts of my biography — that I was a Virginia Law graduate, for example, or that I had recently married, or that my father was also a downtown lawyer — than I would have expected from one so impersonal. Perhaps this was only his prodigious memory; perhaps, had I been reported dead one morning, he would simply have shaken his head at this further example of the inefficient instability of the human estate and telephoned to the managing partner for a replacement. And would that not have been the reaction, however more disguised, of the majority of men?

I had to face the fact that what really disturbed me

about Abel Donner was my suspicion that his bleak vision
of the world might be a truer one than mine. All my adult
life I had been haunted by what I hoped was the merely
neurotic fear that art was illusion and law reality, and
that law was more "real" in direct proportion to its bleak-
ness. And poor Mr. Donner, it struck me in my darker
moods, seemed the personification of that grim fantasy.

It was for this reason, no doubt, that at our lunches I
kept putting questions to him about the one topic whose
bright colors and occasional scandals even he could not
avoid: his clients the Thornes. This was the clan descended from Josiah Thorne, an early accumulator of
Manhattan real estate, now managed by a family corporation with whose legal problems I assisted Mr. Donner. It
was thus that I had become familiar with the many marriages of Harry Z. Thorne, the many traffic tickets of Mrs.
Thorne Leslie, the many bad checks of Oswald Thorne
Plunkett, and other domestic malfunctions. Although
these caused my senior his customary head shakes, there
was a difference. A Thorne peccadillo was not as others;
to him it had a peculiar dignity.

The Thornes had to be protected not only from the consequences of their peccadilloes, but from all the marauders
whom money attracts, particularly the matrimonially
minded. It sometimes seemed odd to me that Mr. Donner
should take it so serenely for granted that no one of either
sex would care to wed a Thorne for aught but financial

advantage. Did it conceal some repressed scorn of his favorite family?

When Alda Thorne, lovely daughter of Simeon, the tribal chief, became engaged to Jason Parrish, brilliant young author of the romantic best-selling novel *Western Wagon*, as amiable as he was attractive and actually a friend of mine, I was startled at the violence of Mr. Donner's reaction. When I mentioned the subject at lunch, he stared grimly across the table at me and announced, "I'm afraid this one's going to be the worst of all."

"But he's been called a genius by the critics!" I protested. "He'll probably sell his book to the movies for a bundle. And he hasn't been married before, and he's not an alcoholic, like so many writers. What more do you want?"

"I'll tell you just what I want. I want a plain honest man with a steady job, preferably in a profession. Someone whose head isn't always in the clouds. This fellow has made just enough money to persuade Alda he's not after hers."

Indignation made me bold. "And what makes you so sure he is, sir?"

"Because these writing and painting guys have just enough sense to know the difference between the money they're bound to blow and a fortune in trust that'll always take care of them."

"Aren't you being just a bit hard on us writers, Mr. Donner?"

This pulled him up a bit, for he was never consciously

unkind. "But you only do it on the side. That's different. With you it's a form of relaxation, like golf. Your real life is law."

I supposed that he meant this as a compliment. Had he spoken his true mind he would probably have classified my writing as a minor personal ailment that it was politer not to mention.

"There are writers who have made regular incomes and lived perfectly respectable lives." I paused to think of authors of whom even he might approve. "Howells. James. Mrs. Wharton." But his stare was not receptive. Had he ever heard of them? "Lord Tennyson," I added desperately.

"Wasn't James an expatriate?"

I abandoned this tack. "And, besides, Jason is a man of sterling character."

"How do you know that?"

"Because he happens to be a friend of mine."

Mr. Donner's frown at once disappeared. Obviously my endorsement of the future Thorne in-law had now been set aside as prejudiced. But his manners were too good to permit of further disparagement.

"Well, anyway her trust is watertight. The principal can't be touched without the consent of *all* the trustees."

Of whom, of course, he was one.

I assumed that Alda's father agreed with his lawyer. The president of the family corporation was a surly and disagreeable man, dark and heavyset, with a reputation for heavy but controlled drinking. He gave as little of his time as possible to managing the family real estate, and I suspected that his abrupt, impatient way of presiding at meetings, his constant petulant interruptions, his drumming on the table, and his throat clearings were designed to get the business over with as quickly as possible, before the basic thinness of his knowledge of its details should become apparent to all present. If he was always accusing others of failing to distinguish the forest from the trees, it might have been because he saw neither.

His relationship with Mr. Donner put me in mind of a historical precedent: that of Louis XIII with his great minister, Richelieu. I suspected that, like the French monarch, Thorne detested the man whose genius was indispensable to the management of his business and would gladly have cashiered him had he been able to find an even remotely comparable substitute. But if Mr. Donner was aware of this — and I could hardly believe he wasn't — he gave no sign of it. He took not the slightest notice of his client's grumbling or of his impatient gestures, simply explaining points of law to him in his dry monotone and pointing out the places where Thorne was to sign.

On the day when Mr. Donner had at last to face his client's resentment of the legal talent that kept him rich, Alda Thorne and her fiancé were sitting with him and me, reviewing the documents for the transfer of title to a building in which she had a major interest. The closing was to take place in an hour's time in one of the firm's conference rooms where her father was to join us. Alda was a charming and vivacious girl with no interest in the business at hand. I could tell by the way she leaned over the document that Mr. Donner was explicating, her head down and held still, that she wasn't hearing a word he said. Jason, on the other hand, whose merry brown eyes and high cheerful laugh and boyish blond looks appeared to deny the idea of a serious author, showed a lively interest in everything, from Mr. Donner to the big bare room to the papers so neatly stacked on his desk. He seemed to be trying to make a party of the occasion.

"I suppose you're planning to have a real estate closing in your next book," Mr. Donner had greeted him, not unamiably, when Jason had surprised us by turning up with Alda. "Well, we'll try to make it as dramatic as we can, won't we, Daniel?"

This was about as friendly as Mr. Donner could be, and it evidently exhausted his efforts at hospitality, for he turned at once to the papers on his desk. After a time even Jason saw that the occasion was not going to yield to his ideas of festivity, and he lapsed into a benign silence until Mr. Donner glanced at his clock.

"I guess the buyer and his counsel should be here any minute. What's holding your father up, Alda?"

"Oh, didn't I tell you? Dad's not coming. He's going to the races at Belmont this afternoon. And you know how he is about *them*."

Mr. Donner retracted his head in shocked surprise. "How about his affidavit of debts and taxes? We can't close without it."

"Oh, that must be what he told me to give you." Alda

took from her purse a sadly crumpled paper and handed it to him. "Is this it?"

Mr. Donner, frowning at its state, glanced over it. "This is it, all right, but it's not notarized."

"I think he said someone in your office could take care of that."

Mr. Donner shook his head emphatically. "Your father should know I don't permit that. He's got to swear to it in the notary's presence. Has he left for Belmont yet?"

"If not, he's just about to. And all hell will break loose if he misses even one race."

"I can't help that. I'll call him."

"I don't mind notarizing it for Mr. Thorne," I volunteered, anticipating a crisis. "I know his signature."

There was an odd little spark in Mr. Donner's pupils that I had not seen before. "You will do no such thing, Mr. Ruggles," he enjoined me formally. Then he picked up his telephone and instructed his secretary to call Mr. Thorne. In seconds the connection was made, and I listened apprehensively as my partner explained to his client about the affidavit.

"I know you're on the way to the races, Simeon, but you'll have to take care of this first. If you want this deal to close, that is. — No, it can't be postponed, not safely anyway. — Because the buyer put a time-is-of-the-essence clause in the contract, and he's looking for any excuse to get out of the deal. — Why? Because real estate prices are dropping; you know that. — No, Simeon, I *won't* ask a notary to do that; he could lose his license. — I don't *care* that you'll make it up to him; you can't make it up to *me*. It's my office, and that's the way I do things. I'm afraid that's final. — I mean it, Simeon! You can either come down here or I'll send a notary to you with the affidavit.— Oh, you're coming right down? — Good."

By the time Thorne got here, we had been in the conference room with the buyer and his counsel, making the closing adjustments, for half an hour. I doubt that I've ever seen an angrier man. He paid no attention to anyone but Mr. Donner when he burst into the room, taking his stand at the end of the long table and shouting down it to his offending lawyer:

"This is the worst goddam outrage I've ever known! Making me come down here to swear before some two-bit notary! There isn't a law firm in this city that wouldn't perform so minor a service for an important client. What the hell sort of crazy kick do you get, Donner, out of humiliating me this way in public?"

But Mr. Donner was imperturbable. He turned to me. "I think Mr. Thorne is ready to attest. Will you kindly act as his notary?" He turned back to his irate client. "Do you swear, Mr. Thorne, that the contents of this affidavit are true and do you acknowledge this signature to be yours?"

Thorne was silent for a moment, as if stunned by such coolness. "I swear," he said at last.

Mr. Donner nodded. "Then we need not detain you further. I hope you will be on time for at least one race at Belmont."

Thorne strode to the door, but turned back to face the room before leaving. "And don't think I shan't be looking for a more obliging lawyer! *He* shouldn't be hard to find."

After the closing I invited Alda and Jason to lunch with me at my club, but as Alda had an appointment with her hairdresser uptown, Jason and I went without her. At our table he ordered a cocktail and raised his glass to toast Mr. Donner. He seemed actually elated.

"He's marvelous! Would any other lawyer treat an important client that way?"

"Most firms have obliging notaries, I guess. And the attorney in charge usually looks the other way. It's really not that big a deal. But then Mr. Donner is a rule to himself."

"And he wasn't even *tempted*, that's what struck me so. He was absolute granite! Would anything in the world, do you think, have induced him to have that paper improperly notarized?"

"Perhaps if someone had threatened Mrs. Donner's life."

Jason's brown eyes gleamed with enthusiasm. "And don't you see how rare that is? A thing to him is either right or wrong, and there's no decision to be made about it! He's like an early Christian, before they started squabbling about the coexistence of the Trinity. One who knew just what he had to do or not to do. So firmly that it didn't matter whether the result was going to heaven or to the lions — or both. Do you suppose he's a saint?"

"Isn't there another side to that? Mightn't he throw *you* to the lions with the same impassivity, if he believed it was right?"

"Of course!" Jason was so delighted at the idea that I could only suppose he had already conceived of a story or novel about my partner. "He would burn you at the stake, like the Grand Inquisitor, without a qualm."

"What becomes of your saint, then? Do saints do that?"

"I rather think they do. Saints can't afford to be sentimental."

"Then we should thank God there are no more of them."

"Perhaps not God. Anyway, it's exciting to run into a man who still *cares*. We're all so wishy-washy."

I thought we had extracted all that the subject held for us. "It really must take a master novelist to find so much to be excited about in a man as colorless as Mr. Donner."

"Oh, to me he has all the colors of the rainbow!"

The episode of the notarization was not followed by the firing of Arnold & Degener. Mr. Donner never referred to the incident, but only two months afterward he asked me to work on a tax problem connected with one of Simeon Thorne's trusts. I had supposed that the unraveling of the latter's long representation by Abel Donner had proved too arduous a task to justify the indulgence of his spleen, and no doubt this had been a factor, but I learned later from my friend Jason, now married to the lovely Alda, that he had persuaded his bride to intercede with her angry parent.

"She wanted me to get Mr. Donner to apologize to her old man. I told her that if Mr. Donner was a man to do that, he wasn't the man for us."

"And she agreed?"

"I don't know that she exactly agreed. But she went along. And old Simeon soon thought better of it. Well he might! That family would soon go to pieces without Donner. He isn't just a lawyer, you see. He's the *law*. He's the iron frame that holds up all their silly banging doors and windows, all their gilded cornices and scallops and capitals. The whole baroque edifice would collapse in a cloud of dust without him."

I shrugged. Obviously, Jason *was* putting my partner and the Thornes in a novel. Still, it was amusing to think of the sober and orderly Mr. Donner united in a book with that crazy gang — rule and misrule, substance and void, the one and the many. Death and life? But which was death, which life? Either way the attribution seemed ironic.

To Jason, anyway, the game seemed more than an intellectual one. He insisted that he would now make a real friend of Abel Donner. He took Alda's place at any family conference at our office and asked all sorts of questions about the deal in point, which Mr. Donner would patiently answer, and then he would invite us all to lunch at a restaurant where he would seat himself next to Mr. Donner and illuminate him about books and authors and the literary world.

"The only way I'll ever get him talking about himself," Jason explained to me, "is by boring him until he *has* to interrupt."

To my astonishment I noticed that Mr. Donner *did* seem to be gradually thawing. Once he observed to me that Jason appeared to be a "likable enough chap." At another time he said, "Jason Parrish is coming down to lunch with me today. Care to join us?" And at his club he took the lead in the conversation and talked, not about rapid transit or reservoirs, but about one of his own early cases where he saved a well-known killer from the electric chair. He was even interesting, almost exciting. But the most remarkable thing of all was when I spotted a copy of *Western Wagon* on his desk. He was actually reading a novel!

Jason carried matters a step further. He and Alda asked my wife, Alice, and me to a dinner of ten in honor of the Abel Donners. They had the reputation of hardly ever going out, but they came, and Mr. Donner, after a period of constraint, relaxed under the influence of the cocktails and the deference paid him by the younger guests (probably tipped off by their host in advance) and told with actual gusto some more tales of his early criminal practice.

After dinner I sat in a corner with Mrs. Donner and discussed with her this new friendship between her husband and our host. She was frankly enthusiastic about it.

"That young man could charm a bird off a tree. It's wonderful that he's so taken with Abel. I suspect my husband has always hankered for the friendship of younger men. He wanted a son terribly, I know, though he was always too kind to mention it to me."

"You mean Jason has been the only one to see that?"

"Perhaps."

"And that *I* could have been such a friend?"

Mrs. Donner's kind, lined brown face became almost grave. "Oh, yes, Daniel. And still could. Abel has talked to me a lot about you."

I felt a twinge of pain with my surprise, and an odd sudden jealousy (was it really that?) of Jason. "What has he said?"

"That he hopes you won't give up the law again. He feels that your two disciplines are now in harness and that it would be a mistake for you to give up either one. He told me that some of your partners think you'd be a better lawyer if you gave up the distraction of writing. But he feels, and I agree with him, that you wouldn't give the time you saved to the law. You'd just give it to fretting over what you'd done."

For a moment I was afraid there would be tears in my eyes. That this old couple, whose feelings about myself I had always assumed were at the most neutral, should have discussed the vital problem in my life and analyzed it with such understanding and sympathy, was profoundly moving.

"You can tell him that I never will leave the law!" I said almost fiercely. "And bless you both for caring!"

Some weeks later Mr. Donner and I were supervising the closing of the passage of title to some out-of-state property belonging to the Thornes. One of the pieces was in Alda's name, and the state law required Jason to release his rights of curtesy to it. I had prepared the document and sent it to him for execution, and he had said he would bring it to the closing. That morning, however, he had telephoned to say he had to fly to Hollywood about a possible movie sale, and that he would send the release by messenger. We had just about finished our business when the messenger hurried in with the envelope.

"Is that the release?" Mr. Donner murmured to me. "I was beginning to wonder if our friend Jason had forgotten us."

I opened the envelope and examined the paper. Then, silently, with a suppressed smile, I handed it to my chief. After a glance he frowned and leaned over to whisper to me, "There's a novelist for you! He's forgotten to have it notarized. Be a good boy, Daniel, and take it outside and notarize it. Don't let anyone see you, though."

"Oh, Mr. Donner, I couldn't do *that*."

He gave me a fierce little glare. "There'll be a devil of a row if this thing has to be postponed. And poor Jason's father-in-law will give him hell. Can't you do a little favor like that for him? I thought you two were such pals."

"Really, sir, it shocks me that you should even ask such a thing."

Mr. Donner now used a word I hadn't dreamed was in his vocabulary. "I didn't think you'd be such a candy ass."

I was now having a thoroughly good time. "But you, more than anyone else, sir, should know I've been trained by a *master*."

Ah, now he got it! I thought I could make out what was almost a blush on that round, bland physiognomy. Had he allowed a featherweight like Jason to cause so much as a ripple in the smooth flow of his seventy-year-old stream? Or was it simply my fantasy, and he did not even recall the other notarial incident? But I still, anyway, suspected that Jason was having the gall to experiment with my new friend, that he was giving him this test to see if he could take him out of his silly novel and put him back in ordinary life. Well, he was not going to get away with it while I was around.

Mr. Donner turned to the others, who had been watching our whispered conference.

"I am afraid, gentlemen, that we shall have to postpone this closing. Mr. Parrish's release is not notarized."

I jumped to my feet. "But it's possible that Mr. Parrish is still in town and could come down here. Let me call him."

I hurried out to the hall and dialed Jason's number on the receptionist's telephone. It rang and he answered at once, as I had been almost sure he would.

"You didn't have that release notarized. How soon can you get your ass down here?"

"Won't Donner let you do it?"

"Of course he won't! You of all people should know that!"

"I thought he might make an exception for me."

"Because you've made such an obvious play for him? Dream on, kid. Mr. Donner makes exceptions for no one. I'll see you in this office in half an hour."

Jonathan Sturges

I HAD KNOWN Jonathan Sturges, curator of drawings at the Empire State Gallery of Art, around town for a number of years before he and I did any actual business together. I use the term "business" because he was not a client but a client's consultant. He accompanied Leonora MacDowell when she came to my office to draft the will that was to dispose of the great art collection that she and her recently deceased husband, Herbert, had put together.

Jonathan and I, as rather persistent bachelors, had met frequently at dinner parties in East Side Manhattan, and we had formed a habit of exchanging pleasantries, often sufficiently withering ones, as we regarded, perhaps too sardonically, the passing parade. On occasion we dined together at a club. He was the best company imaginable, as good a listener as he was a talker, witty, sympathetic, and possessed of a large bag of delightful and sometimes even thought-provoking anecdotes of social doings in Gotham. He was also a first-class art historian with an eye renowned for its impeccable taste. But he was a hard man

to know intimately. He seemed to reserve his inner self
for the beautiful ladies, always slightly older, of whom,
in a long series, he had been from time to time the assidu-
ous companion. A lover? No one was ever sure. He was
cast usually more in the role of the Gallic *soupirant*. And
he seemed to be always on excellent terms with the husbands. Jonathan, unlike many of his profession, had a
knack with tycoons.

Leonora MacDowell was his current inamorata, if that
is the word, in 1960 when she chose Arnold & Degener
to be her counsel after the retirement of her old family
lawyer. It was an important event in my life. I was married now and a partner in the firm, and this was my first
"megestate." I responded only soberly to Jonathan's jovial,
conspiratorial wink when he walked jauntily into my
office behind the lovely widow.

Leonora was probably fifty at the time; Jonathan and
I, who were the same age, some seven or eight years
younger. She was tall and thin and infinitely elegant,
with long blond hair and large sad eyes. She went in for
big jewelry, for gold, for things that jangled with her
constant nervous movements: the taking out of a compact
for a quick dab at her nose, the insertion of a cigarette in
a holder, the lighting of it, the almost immediate putting
it out. She was shrewd, concise, quickly bored, very definite about what she wanted. If she peered into her compact mirror after she made a statement, it was to give you
a moment to take it in, not to question it.

"I have asked Jonathan to come today because he has

had some part in the formation of my plan. I know that you and he are friends and should be able to work together. The basic idea is this. I have decided to bequeath the whole collection to the Empire State Gallery." Out came the Fabergé case. A cigarette was extracted. Snap. The closed lid pronounced an Amen. "*But.* Oh, yes, there's a very big but." Out came the lighter. Pfit! "The museum must house it independently in what is to be called the Herbert and Leonora MacDowell Wing." Here a long inhale of the weed. "The estate will pay for the wing, of course. But. And here's an even bigger one. The wing will contain rooms that are as nearly as possible duplicates of the rooms now housing the collection at 740 Park Avenue. It is my purpose that it be displayed intact."

Jonathan now came in as if on cue, with a seemingly prepared statement delivered in a lilting tone that was almost (or perhaps really) a parody of itself. "Leonora and I believe that too much art is exhibited in museums today as if it had sprung like Minerva from the brain of Jupiter. Why was this or that artifact created? And for whom? The plaque might tell you, but who reads a plaque? The viewer has no way of *seeing* that Titian, say, or El Greco, painted either for palaces or churches, to inspire respect for great persons or awe of God. Leonora, of course, does not wish to recreate a chapel for her Piero or a *salle des glaces* for her Nattier, but she and I heartily agree that the juxtaposition of beautiful paintings with beautiful furnishings can create a more fitting ambiance for their display. I should be tempted to go even further and suggest that a great collection such as Leonora's and Herbert's has an artistic unity of its own, so that its preservation as such, far from being a mere memorial to a pair of magpies, may be the enshrining of a supreme work of human imagination."

The word "magpies" was a clue to Jonathan's persistent independence, always bubbling up over the surface of what otherwise might have seemed sycophancy. Leonora could be brisk and down-to-earth and even very funny, but like so many who come to take for granted the bowings and scrapings of those who envy — or worse — genuinely admire the rich, she at times humbly accepted their homage and tended to speak of her own role as an art collector and philanthropist in a lofty, world-weary tone, as if it were a task imposed on a terrestrial angel who would much rather be twanging her harp amid the anonymous host above. Jonathan's "magpies" acted like a spray of cold water on the emanation of such dreamy moods. One day, I supposed, he would go too far. But did he care?

"Well, my things *do* seem to help each other," she admitted now, as if she had had to be persuaded of this. "When I think of all the trouble Herbert and I took, marrying this chair to that table, or this set of porcelain to that tapestry, it does seem a pity to think of all the divorces that would follow an unrestricted bequest."

"Would the whole apartment go into the wing?" I asked. I knew it was a triplex.

"Well, not the kitchen or the maids' rooms," Jonathan

replied with a chuckle. "Or even Leonora's john, though she does have a Prendergast hanging over it."

"And how do you know *that?*" she demanded archly.

"I slipped into your bedroom at one of your parties to snatch a peek at that divine little Boucher you told me you keep in there. But when the maid who was turning down your bed saw me, she simply pointed to the bathroom door."

"I don't like that at all!" Leonora exclaimed, with the loud rumbling laugh of her less ethereal moments. "I don't see why she should assume, when a gentleman comes to my bedroom, it's for *that.*"

I glanced from one to the other as he joined in her laugh. Many people probably assumed that Jonathan was homosexual and Leonora what is called a "fag hag." The rich, older, fashionable woman and the bachelor with exquisite taste — it seemed a natural setup. But there was something about Jonathan that denied it. He was a small, lively squirrel of a man, with thick short black hair and large, lemurlike eyes, always scrupulously neat and well dressed, who wore his sapphire studs and cufflinks more like a Renaissance princeling than a twentieth-century curator. And there was something uncompromisingly male about his self-sufficiency. He was widely respected in art circles and given full credit for having built up the splendid collection of Italian master drawings at his museum, but he showed no desire to rise further in the world, to become a director, for example, or the head of a university department, or even a writer on art. No, he seemed perfectly content, with a small trust fund to augment his salary, to remain at his post and, in the varied course of his active social life, to advise his rich friends on how best to improve their collections.

Yet it was not, as I could see by the position he occupied that morning, that he was lacking in ambition. It was rather that he nursed a special brand of that quality; he coveted the position of an *éminence grise* in New York's mighty art world. I am sure that his heart beat more rapidly when the chairman of the board of the Museum of Modern Art or the Guggenheim, at a brilliant dinner party after the ladies had retired from the dining room, walked down the table where the gentlemen remained, past magnates and statesmen, to sip his brandy with Jonathan Sturges. And from what he now proceeded to set forth I could see that it was going to give him a decided jag to fight the administration of his own museum.

"Make no mistake about it," he warned us, as if turning to the main order of business, "the real trouble is going to be with our director, Herr Stettin. We shall be flying in the teeth of his announced policy of the non-segregation of gifts. You've heard him: no more isolation of collections, no matter how princely! Everything from cellar to roof, throughout the institution, to be subject to a rigid chronological or geographical scheme. Egypt for the Egyptians; Rome for the Romans; impressions for the impressionists. Life to be made easy for those dreary docents who intone: 'Here you can see the influence of

Manet on Monet, of money on Manet, of Tom on Dick, and of Dick on Harry.' All art to serve as footnotes to the theses of the students of the great Stettin. *Achtung!*" Here Jonathan leaped to his feet and shot out his arm in a fascist salute.

"Dearie, be serious," Leonora reproached him. "Remember that Dan's meter is running."

"But I've never been more serious!" Then he suddenly shrugged and fell back in his chair. "Anyway, Dan will have to cope with Stettin. For there's no point in his even drafting the will until we have the museum's commitment to accept the bequest with *all* its conditions."

Such indeed, it was at once agreed, would be my first task for the new client, and Jonathan suggested that I call on Dr. Stettin as soon as he returned from a trip to London, the following week. In the interim Jonathan and I met alone, without Leonora, to work out the details of the approaching interview in his delightful jewel of a flat, high over the park on Central Park South, surrounded with Venetian furniture and Renaissance Florentine drawings.

"The essential thing," Jonathan pointed out, "will be for you and me and Stettin, assuming he goes along, to prepare a detailed plan for the new wing before it's submitted to Leonora. She likes to do things on the pounce, and she might just jump at a fait accompli."

"But won't we need her input?"

"It's precisely what we will not need. I don't say that Leonora doesn't have an eye. How could she not have, trained as she has been, by a master?" Here Jonathan made me a little bow, as if modestly acknowledging my applause. "But it's hard for rich collectors not to have their heads turned. The combination of the unctuous flattery of the dealer who's just cheated them with the shrieks of gaping dinner guests who want to please their host, is strong stuff. Leonora suffers from the illusion that the presence of an artifact in her collection is in itself a guarantee of its worth. And from there it's an easy step to the illusion that the presence of *any* object in the Mac-Dowell apartment is a guarantee that it's a masterpiece."

"Well, I guess I'll have to leave that battle to you and Dr. Stettin."

"No, my dear fellow, you must do *your* part. Your job will be to make any revisions of the proposed plan involve so many boring legal details that she will drop the idea. That shouldn't be hard. Like all great ladies of fashion, Leonora's attention span is minimal."

I smiled. "You forget, Jonathan. Leonora is my client. Not you. And not the museum."

"But I don't want anything that's not in Leonora's best interest! I want the MacDowell collection to be the finest jewel in the museum's crown. And isn't that what *she* wants?"

"But a lawyer shouldn't substitute his judgment of what's best for the client for the client's."

"Who said anything about *your* judgment? I'm asking you to substitute *mine*."

Here he erupted in a shout of laughter. But I knew

that Jonathan was at his most serious when he laughed loudest. "Anyway," he continued, "you won't have to try to be boring. Just be your usual self, old boy."

My conference with Dr. Stettin was not initially successful. I had an immediate apprehension of this by the manner in which he greeted me. I was told that he was supervising the installation of a new show, and when I went to the indicated gallery I had to wait some twenty minutes while he directed workmen who were pushing about large abstract sculptures. I got the idea that he wanted me to recognize that his real work came first, even before the reception of the legal emissary of a powerful trustee. He was a short, muscular man with a very square face and a Teutonic crew cut. When he greeted me at last, his manners were elaborately cordial.

"Ah, my dear Mr. Ruggles, excuse me, excuse me. Duty makes me forget my manners. Shall we go up to my office? This way, please."

A firm clutch on my elbow guided me from the gallery and through two others on our route to the administrative section. In one of these Dr. Stettin spotted a visitor who was feeling the texture of a Chippendale cabinet. He at once released my elbow and strode over to the offender.

"Will you oblige me," he thundered, "by immediately removing your filthy paw from that artifact!"

The startled man jumped away from the cabinet. After a moment, however, recovering himself and noting that his censor was not a guard, he snarled, "And who the hell are you to order me about?"

"I am a member of the public and as such I have a right to protect the collection from abuse."

"I wasn't abusing it, for chris'sake!"

"One touch, multiplied enough times, can discolor the wood. It is not for you to decide which touch."

"Oh, dry up."

"Would you care to accompany me to the director's office? Shall I call a guard?"

"No, no. I was on my way out, anyway."

"Very well." Stettin's eyes sternly followed the retreating figure. "And it may interest you to know," he shouted after it, "that I happen to be the director of this museum!"

As Stettin and I continued on our way, he explained: "I never tell them who I am until I've first subdued them in my capacity as simple citizen."

In his office we sat for half an hour in silence while he carefully read Jonathan's lengthy typescript. It was obvious that he had already heard of Leonora's project; she had certainly made no secret of it to her fellow trustees. At last he looked up.

"Of course, Mr. Ruggles, this plan will be carefully studied by the interested curators and by our museum architect before it is submitted to the board. But I feel it only fair to you and to Mrs. MacDowell to warn you in advance that I should not be readily prepared to recommend to our trustees so massive and abrupt a departure from our recently announced policy and master plan."

As I studied those rigid features, those hard, glazed dark eyes, I was overcome by the sudden conviction that this man was prepared for a fight to the finish. Jonathan had been convinced that his resistance would crumble before the greed of the board for the MacDowell treasures, but I was not so sure. After all, the collection would not go to the museum until Leonora's death, and she was only in her fifties, with two living parents, hale and hearty in their mid-eighties. And furthermore Leonora could always change her will, so that the museum, in agreeing to accept the bequest, would be in the position of throwing to the winds a supposedly fixed and fundamental philosophy at the first flutter of a mere hope. But I had already developed the idea of a counterproposal, dependent, of course, on the sanction of a client as yet unaware of it, and I decided on the spot to try it out. It was vital to put it on the table before the director had painted himself into too tight a corner.

"Let me, Dr. Stettin, put to you a proposition of my own. But one that I have reason to believe might prove at least interesting to Mrs. MacDowell. Suppose you were to announce that because of an exceptional opportunity — one never likely to occur again, the chance, so to speak, of a lifetime — you had taken it upon yourself to adopt the initiative of recommending to your board one great and final qualification to the general rule."

Oh, how those dark eyes stared at me now! "And that would be?"

"That the MacDowell collection would come to you *now*. To be installed in a new wing constructed under your and the donor's supervision."

In all decency I should draw a curtain over the director's deliberations. Only I had a peek at the agitation that betrayed the inner struggles. For after all, what my proposal, if implemented, would ensure was that the greatest single gift of the century to the Empire State Gallery of Art would have come in the administration and presumably through the solicitation of Franz Stettin! It was irresistible.

Nor did I have much trouble with my client. Leonora was already concerned at the mounting thefts of masterpieces and the wisdom of living in an apartment that was virtually an art museum. Under my plan she would have her rooms where she could see them whenever she wished, for I would stipulate that she was to have access even on days when the public was not admitted, and she would have the additional delight of supervising the installation and seeing that every detail was in accord with her wishes. My final argument was that, once installed, it could never be changed.

"Courts have considerable leeway in determining the 'intent' of a donor after his death. But in your case there will be no question of what your intent was, because every object will have been put in its exact place by you!"

"Dan, you're a great lawyer," she assured me, and I wondered what was the largest fee that could be charged for preparing an *inter vivos* gift.

I had been a bit uneasy as to what Jonathan's reaction to the plan would be, but I was not at all prepared for its violence. I found him waiting in the reception hall of my firm when I arrived at half past nine one morning. He jumped up without a word of greeting as soon as he saw me and followed me down the corridor to my room.

"Do you realize that Leonora is planning to donate the whole damn collection *now*? This very year?" He was almost shouting as I stood before my desk turning over my mail.

"Of course I realize it."

"And do you remember what I said about her not being able to distinguish the good from the bad, when it was a question of her own possessions?"

"Sit down, Jonathan, and let's discuss this thing rationally. Do *you* remember what *I* said about a lawyer's job being simply to implement his client's intent?"

"He can't guide it? He can't moderate it?"

"Within reason. But I really can't see that I have any role to play in the plans for the MacDowell wing. That is something to be worked out between Leonora and the director. My job is done when I've prepared the deed of gift and appraised the tax consequences."

"And you don't care that Stettin, his lips slavering at the prospect of immediate glory, will allow her to botch what could be the noblest section of a great museum?"

"Oh, Jonathan, you exaggerate so. Stettin isn't going to do anything like that. And Leonora isn't that extreme."

"Every collector is extreme when it comes to arranging his own things. And Stettin doesn't give a damn. He showed that when he reversed his whole policy the moment he spied his chance to persuade her to make the gift in her lifetime. *And* in his!"

"As a matter of fact it was I who persuaded her."

"You!" Jonathan leaped to his feet as if from a table at which he suddenly realized he had been supping with the Devil.

"Certainly. When I saw that Stettin was never going to agree to the bequest, I asked him if he would feel differently about an outright gift."

"And you call *that* implementing your client's intent?"

"It was a question of finding a way for her to accomplish, as closely as possible, what she wanted to accomplish."

"Plus a way of saving your fee! Lawyers! What whores you are. You don't give a damn about anything but making a fast buck catering to the egos of your rich clients."

His features had congealed as his nervous gesticulations ceased. Jonathan stared at me now with what I was appalled to recognize as actual hate. There was an amazing strength in his small, compact, quivering body.

I tried vainly to soothe him. "Oh, come off it. Things aren't that bad. Anyway, Leonora will probably take your advice about the wing. You've worked together before, haven't you? Go walk around the block and calm down. If you're free, I'll be happy to take you to lunch at noon."

"I wouldn't lunch with you now or any time, Ruggles," he snarled as he abruptly left the room.

He did, however, make an effort to work with Leonora on the plans for the wing, but their partnership bogged down in sorry failure. She complained to me that he had become impossibly bossy, and at last she asked me to tell him that his help was no longer welcome. When I wrote him to this effect, for I did not care to encounter his wrath on the telephone, he returned my letter with the angry legend scribbled across the top, "Of course, she's too yellow to tell me herself. Typical!"

I had to admit that there was some truth in this. Leonora, like many society ladies who enjoyed an amiable reputation for benevolent despotism, could become very evasive at the threat of armed conflict, retreating behind a palace guard of servants, attorneys, and accountants. When, two months later, she telephoned me with the news that Jonathan had insisted on a hearing before the museum's trustees to present his objections to the acceptance of the proposed MacDowell wing, it was to request that I represent her in her absence.

"I shouldn't think you'd want to miss the scene," I told her. "Jonathan will go down with all his guns firing. Of course, he hasn't a prayer of succeeding."

"Then why does he *do* it?" she demanded in what was almost a wail. "It will probably cost him his job. Stettin is absolutely furious. He didn't want to permit the hearing at all, but Jonathan went over his head to his friends on the board. No, of course I don't want to be there. Jonathan will undoubtedly be very abusive. You can tell me about it afterward. Is it *my* fault if he wants to commit suicide?"

It was probably just as well that Leonora did not attend the hearing. It was indeed an extraordinary performance that took place a week later in the board room of the Gallery of Art before some thirty trustees and a sulking director. Jonathan had prepared blown-up photographs of the principal rooms in the MacDowell apartment, with black lines drawn across them to indicate just how and where the public would be admitted. Projecting these on a screen and alternating them with floor plans of the same rooms, he demonstrated exactly how far the viewer would be from each artifact and what obstructions would fall between them. His comments, launched in a sarcastic, scathing tone, went something like this:

"The Rembrandt of the girl with the red parrot, hanging over the Boulle table, is seen at a distance of twenty-two feet and at an angle of forty-five degrees. But what of that? Are there not those who claim that the master is actually better seen from afar? Detail is available to those who bring their opera glasses. And anyway, in this day of changing attributions, how long will it be a Rembrandt? Can't we make out, or mightn't we if we could come just a bit closer, the least little hint of the work of that clever improviser, Boldini père? Never mind. We are more than compensated for distant art by how closely we can approach to this exquisite portrait photograph of Herbert MacDowell by the one, the only, the incomparable Cecil Beaton? And what an enchanting thing it is to be able to wander free of the cavernous impersonality of the modern museum amid the warm reminders of a uniquely civilized family life! What have we here? A divan, signed, a genuine W. and J. Sloane piece, as early as 1920. How many of *those* will you see in a run-of-the-mill cultural institution? If I could make *one* suggestion, one hint that imperfection is still a possibility, I might plead with our imaginative director to move the Houdon bust of Count Vergennes a little to the left so that we could have a better vista of the likeness of the beautiful Leonora by our great soldier-painter, Dwight D. Eisenhower."

I began to understand, as Jonathan continued his spiel, striding up and down the little platform before the screen, writhing like Kaa, the rock python in *The Jungle Book*, before the hypnotized apes he is about to devour, that he had lost all intention, had he ever had any, of defeating Leonora's project. What he was simply doing was chanting a hymn of hate, pouring out the resentments of his years of subservience to a society that he deemed pretenders only to the worship of art, one that preserved its true reverence for decoration and that only when it complemented wealth. How he must have despised all the hosts and hostesses whose taste he had helped to form; how he must have envied them their ability to acquire a room full of masterpieces as easily as he could buy one drawing by Carracci or Giulio Romano! He must have seen himself as one of the lonely but privileged few to whom has been vouchsafed the sense of true beauty, but who are obliged to pay for that bounty by coming to terms with insensitive accumulators like the MacDowells or ambitious pedants like Stettin. And now he proceeded to fling even those terms to the winds by declaring that he preferred Savonarola's bonfire of vanities to Leonora's mausoleum of them!

At last there was an indignant question from the stupefied audience.

"Haven't collectors always wanted some recognition of

their efforts and generosity? What about the figures of the donor we see in so many Flemish sacred paintings?"

"And how is the donor depicted?" Jonathan retorted in a tone of near glee. "On his knees, with all the warts on his fat Flemish face showing! But I grant you, he was still the forerunner of the magnate of breakfast foods who wants his bust beside that of Michelangelo in the Pantheon of Art. Neither has any true connection with the great collectors of the golden ages: Lorenzo the Magnificent, or Charles the First, or Cardinal Mazarin. These identified art not with themselves but with the civilizations over which they presided and of which they were the living symbols!"

There had never been any serious prospect that he would prevail, and after the meeting few, even among his friends on the board, cared to come over to acknowledge his efforts. The alliance of the museum administration with a principal trustee and donor had made acceptance of the MacDowell wing a matter of dogma; it was heresy to make mock of the popular and venerated Leonora, acknowledged high priestess of the cultural and financial establishment. I lingered while he exchanged some words with the handful that greeted him and then came over to stretch out my hand. Somewhat to my surprise he took it.

"You were great," I assured him. "It was like one of those noble perorations at the end of a Paul Muni movie where he played Zola or Darrow."

Jonathan grinned. "You may be a lackey, Dan, but you're a nice lackey."

"What'll you do now?"

"Oh, quit before they axe me. Though maybe they won't dare axe me for a bit. There are other ways of making a curator's life miserable. I shan't wait around to give them the chance."

"I don't suppose so vivid a show of independence will have endeared you to the world of the cultural institutions."

"Don't be too sure. Fashion is king. And every so often it becomes fashionable to smile on independence. Not all the world loves Stettin and Leonora."

And he was right. He got a job almost immediately as curator of European painting in the Museum of Art in Rochester. But I have recently heard that he may be on the way out there, too. Apparently he persuaded one of their biggest benefactors to give his great Rubens, the *Dormition of the Virgin*, to the Empire State Gallery of Art!

"It really belongs more in that collection," he was quoted in the press as saying. "It's a twin of their *Assumption of the Virgin*."

Aunt Lou Haven

SHE WAS NOT a real aunt. She was one of those old maids (that term again!) who was called "Aunt Lou" by many of the children of her friends, who was included in family parties even on such intimate occasions as Christmas Eve, and who was popular for her general benevolence, her handsome presents, and her ability to act as a mediator in the disputes between the generations.

She was a woman of means, though not so much as we all had thought. When she died, she left a small estate, indubitable evidence that she had not hesitated to dip into her capital. Why not? An only child herself, she had left no posterity. Her modest share of an old New York clipper ship fortune could not have been better spent than maintaining her small cluttered apartment in the East Fifties with its bookcases crammed with fine editions and its tables and vitrines full of Greek and Roman bronzes and Byzantine ivory carvings. Nor was it all inanimate. Flora were represented by large potted azalea plants and bowls of chrysanthemums; fauna by the blue and yellow macaw on a perch, never caged, two canaries, a tank of jewel-like fish, a spaniel, and a large pink Siamese cat. Aunt Lou had no need of a decorator's harmony. Beautiful things and beings, she said, should be good enough for one another. They were certainly good enough for her.

I knew her from my childhood, but I tend to think of her as in her mid-fifties, when I was in college, tall and thickset, but not stout, with a square marble face, a high noble brow, and blond hair (it never grayed) pulled straight back to a knot behind. But it was always evident that she conceived of herself as more ethereal, more romantic anyway, than this rather solid physical presence suggested. The plain long dresses that she affected had a priestess note; her tan, gazing eyes seemed to be looking beyond you, not inattentively, but as if to relate your discourse to something higher, and her voice, when she spoke of the mysteries of art or music, had a husky, reverent note. Her bookplate by Maxfield Parrish showed a young, epicene figure seated on a stone wall before a forest background, an open volume in hand, the fine Greek profile raised to suggest a mystic contemplation of some passage just read. It bore the legend, "He serves all who dares be true."

Of course, she wouldn't have so appealed to young people had this been all. She had a sense of humor so strong that it threatened at times to send shivering cracks through the whole edifice she had been to such pains to create. There was no more devoted opera buff, yet she nudged me once at a performance of *Norma*, when we were seated so far to the side as to see around the singers, to point out that Rosa Ponselle, her back to the audience, was taking advantage of her position to snatch a sip from the goblet that she was ostensibly raising to the gods, and gargle. And then Aunt Lou's whole frame had fairly throbbed with suppressed laughter. Her gravest moments were constantly being so interrupted. Those little scoundrel imps, Meredith's "dogs and pets of the comic spirit," seemed to be actually inside her rather than hungrily watching from without.

She had been christened Louise, but she hated the name, which to her denoted a rather saccharine femininity, and she preferred the blunt masculine abbreviation. Which brings up at once, in our day, the question of her sexual preference. She was supposed, as a debutante, to have been briefly and unhappily engaged to a rather colorless man, and that was all, as far as males were concerned. As to women, she had many deep and emotional friendships, but I think she was always too New York for a "Boston marriage." I remember her many comments on the good looks of some of her friends: "Elizabeth threw back her beautiful head and laughed," or "Elaine blinked her sapphire eyes at me," but I doubt very much that she ever went further. She would have been restrained by the stiffer inhibitions of her generation and by her own attraction to just the sort of woman least likely to respond. But I shall come back to this. One almost has to, these days.

Aunt Lou professed no other god but beauty. Animals

and plants, she claimed, were naturally endowed with it. Man could never hope to excel the soaring albatross, the bird of paradise, the black panther, the jaguar. Humans, both male and female, boasted some fine examples, to be sure, but the majority had to seek beauty, if they desired it, more in art than in themselves. For Aunt Lou it was found in opera (she had heard *Tristan* fifty times; a stack of old programs attested to the fact), in impressionist painting (she had somehow been able to afford a tiny Renoir and a Sisley), in English poetry and fiction, in Walt Whitman and in Emily Dickinson.

At an early age I found her an ally against my parents' more prosaic view of the world. When I was very small, I can remember her saying, in the very teeth of Mother's injunction that I should eat my carrots, "If I were you, Dan, I should make a resolution, right here and now, never to allow one drop of liquid or one morsel of nourishment to pass my lips that I did not want."

She got away with this under the exemption afforded to "characters." Even Mother let it pass. Aunt Lou was a few years older than Mother and had been an "inherited" friend, one of the young women who had admired my very popular Grandmother Fisher, and she tended to embrace us Ruggleses as a unit, seeking to make up to any of us what that one failed to get from the others. She saw me as the artist of the family, and I adored her for this, even while I trembled that her theory might be taken as a kind of hubris by our household gods. At boarding school I used to send her the stories I wrote for the *Cheltonian*.

"You're one of the lucky ones," she told me gravely. "I'd give all my remaining teeth and the five fingers of my left hand to have half of what you've got. Don't think it will be easy, though. You'll have to give up a lot of things that a lot of people find very important."

In those Depression years it was possible for persons of very small means to indulge an artistic bent and still live attractively. At worst one could go to Paris or Rome. These so-called sacrifices seemed glamorous to me. In our own day of high costs, when the alternative to the mundane job may be poverty, we are wrong to accuse young people of materialism.

"Oh, I shouldn't mind *that*," I exclaimed, seeing myself already scribbling at a table outside a Paris café, an absinthe by my pad, a vision of gray façades and chestnut trees before me. "But suppose I should find I had no real talent?"

Aunt Lou looked up quizzically at her macaw, which simply raised a claw to scratch its eyelid. "Ah, you're your mother's child. You must learn to gamble, my boy."

It was a mistake on my part to relate this quip to Mother, but then I could never resist using Aunt Lou as a foil.

"I'd like to know what gamble Lou Haven has ever taken," Mother retorted. "She's never married or had a child. She's never taken any sort of job. So far as I can see, she's simply sat back comfortably on her inheritance and acted as though she were superior to the rest of the world."

Mother was being harsh, but she resented Aunt Lou's

offering what she considered irresponsible advice to an impressionable youth. And then she had never really liked this "inherited friend." Mother was loyal to any relationship established by the parent whom she had adored, but she couldn't ignore the fact that she and Aunt Lou disagreed on just about every topic.

"Of course, you don't think art is important," I sniffed.

"I think great art is of great importance. I don't 'walk down Piccadilly with a poppy and a lily,' no. And I hope I never confuse real life with the smell of paint on cardboard. It's more than an opera set to me."

Father and Mother were as one in their scorn of Aunt Lou's "sentimental" approach to the arts. Father was even more critical than Mother where music was concerned, for he had the finer ear and detested Aunt Lou's habit of nodding her head to keep time during what he called Verdi's "noisy choruses." When Aunt Lou, who treasured a slight acquaintance with Kirsten Flagstad, told him that the great diva had confessed to three mistakes in a matinee of *Tristan*, one of which Aunt Lou claimed she had caught herself, Father had whispered to me, "Probably not one of them."

"Would great art exist without lesser art?" I asked Mother. "Would we have *Hamlet* and *Lear* without *The Honest Whore* and *The Virgin Martyr*?"

"I couldn't tell you. I'm not fresh from a Chelton course in Elizabethan drama. But would you want to spend your life doing second-rate work to give a first-rater something to exceed?"

In spite of Mother, Aunt Lou's emphasis on the value

of beauty in art and nature helped me to justify my own perception that these things deserved a far greater importance than my parents accorded them. It was unfortunate that Aunt Lou so often played into Mother's hand.

One weekend in New York, in my Yale days, calling on Aunt Lou, I found her much excited.

"Have you heard about the wolves?"

"What about the wolves?"

"At the zoo. Some terrible young men have been climbing over the fence at night and tormenting them. Stoning them! Can you imagine anything more hideous? Well, last night one of them went too far. He got into the enclosure to retrieve a shoe he had thrown — he had run out of stones, I guess — and a wolf got him!"

"And killed him?"

"I'm afraid not. But mangled him badly."

There was a strange glitter in Aunt Lou's eyes as she got up to sway in what appeared to be the suggestion of a weird dance, perhaps a reminiscence of Electra's gyrations after the murder of Clytemnestra in Strauss's opera. I was appalled.

"You shouldn't be so triumphant, Aunt Lou. They'll probably have to put down the wolf."

She was still at once. "For what? For being a wolf? Why don't they put down the boys for being boys?"

"Really, Aunt Lou, whose side are you on?'

"The wolf's! The beautiful wolf's!"

"But in the last analysis, doesn't even the most devoted animal lover have to come down on the side of man?"

"No! All the evil in the world comes from man!"

"I'm not so sure of that." My eye fell on her cat. "Have you ever seen Caesar playing with a mouse?"

She looked quizzically at the animal. "Maybe Caesar's a man."

When I got home I asked Mother if it was possible that Aunt Lou had been drinking. She looked at me sharply.

"So you've found that out."

"Why did you never tell me?"

"Because it wasn't my business to."

"Has it been going on for long?"

"Oh my, yes. Since before you were born. I guess whenever the world seems not *quite* beautiful enough, she takes a nip."

Aunt Lou's drinking, foolish though it may seem, became a factor in my life, for I had allowed her to be too much the symbol of the artistic life, just as I had allowed Mother to be too much the symbol of the practical one. But our psyches, particularly in youth, have a vicious habit of exaggeration; they view the world as a cartoon. Even today, looking back on Aunt Lou, the memory has a rather ginny flavor, which is hardly just. I can see now that Mother, in opposing her influence on me, played her cards with the utmost fairness. She knew that Aunt Lou's bibulousness would give her an undue disadvantage. My trouble was that Aunt Lou's moods of dreamy reflection seemed to have a relation to at least a mild intoxication, even when she had not been drinking at all.

"You ask me why I didn't write myself, Danny? Oh, but I did, you see, just as I warbled and played the piano and violin and even dreamed of ballet. Don't look at me that way, my boy. I wasn't so hefty then; I wouldn't have bust the boards. But everything I did or tried to do seemed to have no function but to intensify my sense of how much better others had done it. Until I ultimately realized, with a blinding light, that *that* was my true function: to take in, to receive the beauty that others had created. Only thus could I share their company!"

Mother gave this sort of sentiment short shrift. She called it "the inertly sentimental condition" and recommended William James's remedy: its immediate, *active* expression in some gesture, even one as small as being nice to a tedious relative or giving up one's seat in a streetcar.

But there is a part of me that still hankers after the inertly sentimental condition, and I still miss Aunt Lou.

Anyone as vulnerable as Aunt Lou was bound to encounter, no matter how carefully the jungle was fenced out, an ultimate predator, and hers came in the form of a man — a sort of man, anyway. For at the age of almost sixty her oldest and dearest friend, Mary Malvern, "Miss Malvern" to a respectful world, decided to abandon her virgin state and become Mrs. Geoffrey Hurd.

Miss Malvern, unlike Aunt Lou, was rich, very rich. She had her own opera box, which she occupied three nights a week, always with Aunt Lou and on occasion with various Ruggleses. She was tall and a bit austere, with rather statuesque good looks, and she had mild, bland good manners that might or might not have concealed strength of character. I later learned that they did not. Miss Malvern was not so much weak as unsure of herself and perennially undecided. She had been brought up to believe that everyone was after her money. It is notorious that such women are apt to marry fortune hunters. It was only odd that it took her so long.

Aunt Lou had a joke that New York was not a worldly city, as proved by its large number of wealthy old maids. "Think of how many there are," she would say, counting on her fingers. "Anne Morgan. Ruth Twombly. Julia Berwind. Edith and Maud Wetmore (two!). Annie Jennings. Helen Frick. Mary Malvern. Will the line stretch out to the crack of doom? Such a state of affairs would never be tolerated by the bachelors of Paris or Rome. Have we no men any more?"

Unfortunately, there was one for Miss Malvern. Geoffrey Hurd was a bachelor of sixty-five, a smallish fellow, always dapperly dressed, though he clung on occasion to old-fashioned "knickers," with a round pot, a high bald dome, a goatee, a hook nose and malicious black eyes. He was a tremendous busybody, specializing in gossip and etiquette, who had served as a sort of *arbiter elegantiarum* to many famous hostesses and who made no secret of his ambition to make his quiet bride a figure in society and pay back the hospitality that he had enjoyed so copiously

over four decades. Yet with all this it was still obvious that
he was a highly intelligent man. One could not help wondering what he might have accomplished in a wider field.
But as a devout Catholic, the intimate of bishops and
archbishops, as one who saw in the splendor of ecclesias-
tical ceremonial the harbinger of the life to come, and in
true faith the forgiveness of all snobbishness, he had no
reason to regret that he might have made more of his
frivolous preliminary existence.

Geoffrey had, from the beginning, made little secret of
the fact that he regarded Aunt Lou as an obstacle in his
social path. His wife wanted to have her old friend with
her at any social gatherings at which she presided, and
Geoffrey, being in no financial position to dictate orders
to the contrary, had to accomplish his purpose by under-
mining the woman he considered his rival. He even tried
to enlist my support.

"I wish you could get your mother, Dan, to persuade
Lou Haven to be less proprietary about my wife. I mean,
coax her not be around *quite* as much as she is. I'm sure
you see what I mean. After all, you have an aesthetic eye.
Mary alone is really a rather magnificent-looking woman.
But when she is seen with Lou, the very fact that they
both have large figures makes Mary appear to share Lou's
bad points. They become just another couple of old
maids."

I was too much younger than he to retort as I should
have liked to, but when I related this to Mother, she really
blew up. However critical she had been about Aunt Lou

in the family, her loyalty was complete where outsiders were concerned.

"Really, Geoffrey is too odious! The other night he leaned over to me at dinner and whispered, 'I know you're aware of the dark shadow in my life.' As if he wasn't sufficiently compensated by Mary's fortune to put up with one of her harmless old friends! Lou can be irritating, but so, God knows, can he. It disgusts me to see him trying to turn *Cranford* into *Othello*."

"Maybe it makes him feel virile. To make a triangle out of a figure of three virgins."

Aunt Lou and the new Mrs. Geoffrey Hurd were both devoted and competent photographers, and on their numerous trips to Europe and Africa they had taken pictures that had formed the bases of some interesting slide shows for their friends. Aunt Lou, of course, was particularly good with animals, and it was after a dinner at the Hurds, when she was showing the slides of a safari that she and Mary had taken in Kenya two years before, that an unfortunate interchange took place between her and Geoffrey.

She had just put on the screen the series she had taken of an angry rhinoceros that had twice charged the jeep in which she was riding. The driver had easily outdistanced the animal, but he had slowed his vehicle enough to allow his intrepid passenger to get some good close-up shots from the rear.

"It is tragic to think that this magnificent creature is in imminent danger of extinction." Aunt Lou's now melancholy tones came to us across the darkened parlor. "It is being ruthlessly sacrificed to a ridiculous superstition. Because some crazy Arabs to the north insist on deluding themselves that the horn contains aphrodisiac material, one of our noblest mammals must disappear from the earth."

Geoffrey Hurd's high sharp voice was now heard from the back of the chamber. "Are you suggesting that it would be less tragic if it were *not* a delusion?"

Aunt Lou's ample figure moved into the light before the screen, seeking her questioner in the audience. "What do you mean by that?"

"I think we'd all like to know if you would feel that the creatures died less in vain if their horns did, in fact, increase the joy of the amorous Arab."

"Certainly not! I'd be tickled pink if every Arab who partook of the ground-up horn were rendered as impotent and sterile as the carcass of the poor beast he had plundered!"

"Very well. Then we can agree that his crime is not compounded by being motivated by a fallacy. I think it important, in such discussions, to keep the issues clear. Let us proceed to consider the remedies. Has the government of Kenya not established game reserves for the protection of endangered species?"

"Of course. But the poaching goes right on. The poverty is so great and the price of the horn so high, it's impossible to stop it."

"And yet, just recently, I believe there has been some talk of another remedy. One they say is bound to work."

"Is that so?"

"So I have heard. And do you know *why* it will work?"

I had an uneasy sense of sudden hostility between the two voices, the high feminine one of the male seeking somehow to trap the deeper one of Aunt Lou.

"How could I know? What's your remedy, Geoffrey?"

"And yet I can't help wondering if you haven't at least a suspicion. I know you ardent conservationists have your ways of ducking facts that are too unpleasant to contemplate. Oh, I don't blame you! It's an unspeakable world that we're trying to save." The bite in that voice was now even sharper. "The unfortunate fact is that the death rate of the rhino will only go down when poachers are shot on sight. Jail means nothing to them; they're too poor to care. The price of the horn is worth any risk but near certain death. So there's your choice, Lou. The survival of your magnificent beast against the lives of a few hundred ignorant and superstitious natives. Choose!"

I felt an impulse to switch on the lights, but I did not act on it. Something in the darkness seemed to paralyze me. I could almost feel Aunt Lou's heavy breathing. Did she feel that the choice was larger than he put it — that ranged against the noble animals which made up so much of the beauty and drama of the Dark Continent was a horde, an infinite horde of malevolent men, either as grossly ignorant and selfish as the horn-loving Arabs or as small and nasty as the smirking Geoffrey?

"Well, there are an awful lot of people," Aunt Lou answered him slowly at last. "And very few rhinos."

"But don't those people have souls?" Geoffrey jumped

up now to turn on the lights as if to flood the room with the illumination of his faith. "And didn't our beloved Leo XIII deny them to the animals?"

"All the more reason the poor animals should be allowed a normal life span," a blinking Aunt Lou retorted.

But now Mary Hurd's sweet placating voice was heard. "Lou, dear, I think there may be some friends here who have misunderstood you. Reassure them, I beg of you. Tell us that you prefer man to beast."

Was it Aunt Lou's sense of betrayal by her oldest friend, or the culmination of her disgust at the creature that friend had married, or a feeling of the hopeless plight of beauty on a globe that was becoming a solid carpet of humans (and what humans!), or simply too many drinks at dinner that made her suddenly retort in a half strangled voice, "I'd shoot every poacher in the continent to save one rhino!"

It was Mother who now rose, beckoning to Father, and took Aunt Lou home.

Aunt Lou went into a decline after that evening, and her drinking increased alarmingly. Eventually she had to spend some months in a sanitarium. When she emerged she was cured of the habit, at least temporarily, but she seemed somehow subdued, muted, and this condition did not change. The friends rallied around, and Mary Hurd persuaded her husband to come to terms with his erstwhile opponent. It was even arranged that the three of them should go on a safari in Kenya the following year.

A friend of Father's who was in the same group reported to me one of his most vivid memories of that trip. It was of a quiet evening by a watering hole, with Aunt Lou regarding intently through binoculars a pride of sleepy lions stretched out on a ridge, while Geoffrey, perched on a campstool amid the tents, drew up a list of guests for a dinner party to mark the opening of the approaching social season in New York.

Superb fiction from
St. Martin's Paperbacks

BRUISED FRUIT
Amy Ephron
_____ 91043-6 $3.50 U.S. _____ 91044-4 $4.50 Can.

SKINNY ISLAND
Louis Auchincloss
_____ 91047-9 $3.95 U.S. _____ 91048-7 $4.95 Can.

DIARY OF A YUPPIE
Louis Auchincloss
_____ 90761-3 $3.95 U.S. _____ 90762-1 $4.95 Can.

THE HONEYMOON
Knut Faldbakken
_____ 91366-4 $3.95 U.S. _____ 91367-2 $4.95 Can.

ARDABIOLA
Yevgeny Yevtushenko
_____ 90034-1 $4.50 U.S.

ANATOMY OF A MURDER
Robert Traver
_____ 91278-1 $4.95 U.S. _____ 91280-3 $5.95 Can.

Publishers Book and Audio Mailing Service
P.O. Box 120159, Staten Island, NY 10312-0004

Please send me the book(s) I have checked above. I am enclosing
$ _____ (please add $1.25 for the first book, and $.25 for each
additional book to cover postage and handling. Send check or
money order only—no CODs.)

Name _____

Address _____

City _____ State/Zip _____

Please allow six weeks for delivery. Prices subject to change
without notice.

FICTION 1/89

LANDMARK BESTSELLERS
FROM ST. MARTIN'S PAPERBACKS

HOT FLASHES
Barbara Raskin
_____ 91051-7 $4.95 U.S. _____ 91052-5 $5.95 Can.

MAN OF THE HOUSE
"Tip" O'Neill with William Novak
_____ 91191-2 $4.95 U.S. _____ 91192-0 $5.95 Can.

FOR THE RECORD
Donald T. Regan
_____ 91518-7 $4.95 U.S. _____ 91519-5 $5.95 Can.

THE RED WHITE AND BLUE
John Gregory Dunne
_____ 90965-9 $4.95 U.S. _____ 90966-7 $5.95 Can.

LINDA GOODMAN'S STAR SIGNS
Linda Goodman
_____ 91263-3 $4.95 U.S. _____ 91264-1 $5.95 Can.

ROCKETS' RED GLARE
Greg Dinallo
_____ 91288-9 $4.50 U.S. _____ 91289-7 $5.50 Can.

THE FITZGERALDS AND THE KENNEDYS
Doris Kearns Goodwin
_____ 90933-0 $5.95 U.S. _____ 90934-9 $6.95 Can.

Publishers Book and Audio Mailing Service
P.O. Box 120159, Staten Island, NY 10312-0004

Please send me the book(s) I have checked above. I am enclosing $_____
(please add $1.25 for the first book, and $.25 for each additional book to
cover postage and handling. Send check or money order only—no CODs.)

Name _____

Address _____

City _____ State/Zip _____

Please allow six weeks for delivery. Prices subject to change without notice.
Payment in U.S. funds only. New York residents add applicable sales tax.

BEST 1/89